BREAKING RIGHT

BREAKING RIGHT

D.A. LOCKHART

The Porcupine's Quill

Library and Archives Canada Cataloguing in Publication

Title: Breaking right / D. A. Lockhart.

Names: Lockhart, D. A., 1976– author.

Description: Short stories.

Identifiers: Canadiana (print) 20200348205 | Canadiana (ebook) 20200348213 |

ISBN 9780889844360 (softcover) | ISBN 9780889848856 (PDF)

Classification: LCC PS8623.O295 B74 2020 | DDC C813/.6—dc23

1   2   3   •   23   22   21

Published by The Porcupine's Quill, 68 Main Street, PO Box 160,

Erin, Ontario NOB 1TO. http://porcupinesquill.ca

Edited by Stephanie Small. Represented in Canada by Canadian Manda.
Trade orders are available from University of Toronto Press.

We acknowledge the support of the Ontario Arts Council and the Canada Council
for the Arts for our publishing program. The financial support of the Government
of Canada is also gratefully acknowledged.

Canada Council   Conseil des arts
for the Arts   du Canada

Canadä

ONTARIO ARTS COUNCIL
CONSEIL DES ARTS DE L'ONTARIO
an Ontario government agency
un organisme du gouvernement de l'Ontario

Ontario

Ontario Media Development
Corporation

For Don Cornelius Belton (1956–2009),
teacher, mentor, friend.

CONTENTS

9 Riding the Rosewater

29 Breaking Right

53 From the Banks of Jeffersonville

71 Won't Be in Hard Luck No More

99 Mothman Returns to Muncie

109 A Golden Hue of Earth

121 Blackford County Lights

129 Etch A Sketch Shaman

157 Acknowledgements

159 About the Author

RIDING THE ROSEWATER

'Like what you did there,' Omer said. He ran his hand along the curve of the door frame like it was Jenny Geffler's ass at the 1983 Morgan County Fair. 'Where you say you got this from?' Omer was greying in his late thirties, potbellied, with eyes too small for his head and a permanent half-grin that let you know he had long ago made up his mind about just about everything.

'Got this?' Smithwick replied. Smithwick was in his late twenties, with boyish looks and long, pulled-back, curly dark hair. He sat on an old paint bucket, smoking a hash-dipped cigarette. His fourth-hand, grease-heavy clothes wouldn't have been out of place on tour with the Grateful Dead in the band's middle, fading years. He watched as Omer examined the skeleton of the hot rod that the two had been working on for the past year. They were in the garage behind Smithwick's house; a grass and gravel driveway ran up the lawn behind him and the street beyond. 'I did got this nowhere. Shaped and patched the whole thing myself. That's why it's taken me so damned long.'

Omer whistled his appreciation, ran his hand along it. 'How long you say?'

'Gotta figure about near a solid sixty-five hours,' Smithwick said. He sounded proud. Omer had not managed to help out with the build over the past few months. The missus and the kids had been on his back too much to let him get away and work with Smithwick.

'It worth it?' asked Omer.

Smithwick paused for a moment between drags. He almost seemed annoyed at the question and lingered over a brief silence. But he knew Omer, understood that what he thought and what he said were two very different things. Omer wanted to say something to agree with the younger, hipper guy, something to impress him. This was Omer's way of checking to see how he should answer. 'Worth it,' he answered. 'What you think?'

'Yeah,' replied Omer. 'Seems good to me.' He moved his gaze to the door frame, traced the lines down to the rest of the hot rod's body. He dared not touch it. The reverence came from the fact that Smithwick had done all the work that Omer wished that he could have done himself. He felt a pang of anger that he had managed little beyond the daily shuffle of a working father with three boys and a wife who refused to work. The entire emancipatory notion of building a hot rod with Smithwick flooded back to him.

'How's that engine block?' said Smithwick.

'Best thing we've got in the last week was a '98 Tempo. Not what this beauty of ours needs,' Omer stammered out. The car had been a writeoff from the flood in Wheelerville a few weeks back. Omer had hoped to get more insurance salvage from the disaster. When nothing but old couches, fridges, stoves and bags of family collectibles poured in to the junkyard, it became apparent to Omer that folks cared more about their cars than their homes. The Tempo was the best of the few automobiles that he had seen. And it was, like every Tempo ever made, a substantial disappointment.

'You checked that Craigslist?' asked Smithwick.

'You telling me 'bout that before.' Omer nodded and returned to a camping chair beside Smithwick at the entrance to the garage. Just past the edge of the yard, an INRD engine rattled and grinded across the top of 11th Street Bridge at a crawl, heading north towards Indy. A college student buzzed by and then under it on a moped. 'But I didn't get round to it,' Omer said.

'Need you to get on that,' said Smithwick. 'We only got so much time to put this together before the Bedford rally.'

The Southern Indiana annual independent car race lacked the glamour and spectacle of the legendary Indianapolis 500, but the

Bedford IU Credit Union Motorsports Rally was the ticket for so many of those Hoosiers born into working class obscurity. A couple thousand dollars and few mentions in the newspapers was just the sort of ticket that a guy working in a junkyard could use. Across the street, Mike, the owner of the Audi and Mercedes repair shop, worked away under the hood of a sedan. As always, he paid the two no attention.

'You say it's real simple?' said Omer. ''Cause I don't care too much for them Internet things and I ain't no wizard with computers.'

Smithwick took a deep haul off his cigarette. He blew a thick cloud of smoke at the passing train and then handed the cigarette to Omer, who took it up without emotion. He pulled deeply from it. 'Ain't no thing,' replied Smithwick. 'Besides, with you having a wife and kids, you best know that learning and changing is something you should be investing in. It's never time to stop at what you know now.' Omer emphatically agreed with Smithwick. He batted away a thick cloud of cigarette smoke. Mike looked up from the car across the street. He shook his head and then returned to work.

———————————

'Exactly how much are you talking?' asked Gretchen. In her mid-twenties, her tousled dirty-blonde hair and arm sleeve tattoo (the Indianapolis skyline surrounded by colourful foliage) made Omer feel out of place, again. She was clearly both tougher and more attractive than him. He had never gotten around to figuring out the Craigslist thing. Instead, he had obtained her name, Gretchen Canada, from a salvage guy he knew from working at the junkyard in Elletsville. They had met at a burger counter not too far from there.

'Been saving here and there,' said Omer. 'So, about $300.'

'What exactly are you trying to build?' replied Gretchen. 'A Kia or a Chrysler? I know life is on the cheap down here in the hills, but that isn't a whole lot of money.' She was from Indy's west side. True to that origin, and to Chauncey's description of her, Gretchen Canada could often find the near impossible for very little. That and she was also roller-derby-girl hot. 'I mean you are building a hot rod?'

'For the Bedford IU Credit Union Motorsports Rally,' declared Omer.

'That a big one?' asked Gretchen.

Omer nodded. 'Been around since 1988. Larry Bird has a car in it most years.'

Gretchen nodded. Clear enough that she wasn't impressed by the famous name drop. 'Don't picture a $300 engine getting you over that finish line any faster than the rest of them,' she said. 'Hook-nosed basketball player or not. You should consider upping your budget.'

'I could get my wife to cook you some dinners,' replied Omer. It was the only thing of value he could think to offer her.

She laughed. 'Doubt your wife knows or wants to know about me,' she answered. 'Besides I am more of a tenderloin at Mug-N-Bun type.' She paused then looked Omer up and down. Her piercing gaze made him feel like he was being sized up with that slow look over and that half-launched confident smile. He recognized the look Mike had often cast his way. It was the look of someone who would always know more about the world than him. 'Tell me about your buddy and just what exactly you two are up to.'

Omer had met Smithwick at least five years back. Omer had moved his wife and kids out of their tiny-ass apartment on the other side of town into a home down the street from his grandmother. Smithwick, his girlfriend and their daughter rented out a house with a big garage in the same neighbourhood. Omer met Smithwick on one of his walks to get away from the mayhem of the boys and his wife in the small shotgun house. They were fast friends as both men had loved the idea of racing cars. While neither had ever done so, Smithwick had the idea of using his high school automotive knowledge to build a hot rod of his own to race. Omer thought building a hot rod was a good thing to get involved in. He saw it as growing his personal horizons in the grassroots portion of the automotive industry. Since he had a job at the junkyard, he had declared that he would provide all the parts required for the endeavour. So Smithwick had given Omer a list of parts that he needed. Over the months he had built a sweet frame and a proper working suspension, and they were just now getting to the engine. Family life had slowed them down in their pursuit. That and the current business success of Smithwick's pizza delivery job. But both men had wanted to change that, finish their passion project, and do so with more than just a rebuilt Ford Tempo engine. Omer had finished his fries and most of his Coke by the time he had finished explaining things.

It was clear to Gretchen that Omer's wife was mostly in the dark about the hot rod. She could also have been in the dark about Smithwick. She believed the woman was at best an afterthought for Omer, an obstacle to overcome in order to do what he really wanted to do. That thing, whatever it was precisely, was most clearly tied up with the hot rod and his buddy. Omer was an honest and simple man the likes of which she had rarely encountered. There was something that drew her to him, like the way the homeliest, laziest dog at the pound attracts a new owner. 'Omer,' said Gretchen, 'I don't believe for a second Larry Bird has a car in the rally, but let me see this hot rod you and your buddy are working on. Then we can talk about what we should do.'

———————

'I at least want to beat Larry Bird's car,' said Smithwick. He was more energized than Omer had seen him in years. He was nearly prone beside the hot rod, pointing out the front axles and bearings to Gretchen. She squatted beside him, a cat examining the prey dropped before her. Omer hung back towards the wide-open garage door. The trees above him whirred with the mid-afternoon serenade of cicadas and tree frogs. Gretchen smiled but said nothing about Larry Bird.

There was a warmth in the way Smithwick had welcomed Gretchen. They seemed to be kindred spirits, and they spoke of the hot rod in ways Omer only marginally understood. While he loved the idea of cars and had come to know the names of the parts, plugs and valves that went into them, Omer had very little practical knowledge of how cars worked, but he knew he would be the one to drive the hot rod when it was done. It was he who would coax their creation across the line in Bedford. He had watched *Saturday Night Thunder, Tradin' Paint, NASCAR Nation* and every other car show he could on ESPN and SPEED in preparation. He knew that Smithwick did not have cable. He knew that Smithwick had little ambition beyond tinkering in his garage.

When Smithwick was done explaining the layout of the hot rod, they convened under the large silver maple that stood at the far, low end of the yard. The three of them sat on the ground, drank sweet tea that Smithwick's girlfriend brought out to them. Gretchen and Smithwick went over the minutiae of the hot rod: the balance of the bearings, the clearance between axles. Omer stared off towards the nearby intersection. The environmental science professor in the corner house was hand-weeding his front garden bed.

'Omer.' Smithwick called him back to attention. 'You figure we could get it moving with a classic engine? A 1970s Ford build or something?'

The question was not something he had considered. He had been awaiting the arrival of a usable engine at the yard. He had figured he would know the right one when he saw it. He considered the bulk of the classic engines, the ancient monolithic Galaxies and 500s, the way they hollered into the sky like old men chasing what they weren't anymore. He glanced at Gretchen, took in her lean, muscular look, so different from him or his corn-fed, three-child wife. The promises offered by post–checkered flag milk was not for the commonplace. They needed something different. Something that said *we need to change things up, become what we've waited to become.*

'Nope,' Omer replied. 'Nothing that old. We really need it to be nimble.'

Smithwick and Gretchen went quiet, surprised to hear Omer express an opinion of his own. Smithwick in particular looked a little concerned, obviously caught off guard to have lost the blind devotion of his most reliable yes-man. After a few moments, Gretchen slowly nodded her head and broke into a smile. 'He's right,' she said. 'Your frame in there is pretty light to be supporting the weight of a classic beast.'

Omer took great pleasure in the agreement of a woman. It was something that he had yet to experience in his twelve years of marriage.

'What do you figure?' Smithwick asked, the question directed at Gretchen more than Omer.

'Something from over there,' Omer replied with hardly a thought. He gestured to Mike's Repair Shop across the street. 'Honda is running good on the Indy Car circuit this year. And they are light.'

'You watch Indy Car?' inquired Smithwick.

'Some people watch computer videos,' said Omer. 'I study Indy Car replays on cable.' He drank deeply from the sweet tea in his hand.

'You two know that guy?' asked Gretchen.

'We do,' replied Smithwick, 'but that's not a good thing. He's stared at us enough without saying nothing. Lets us know he don't like us much.'

'Called us rednecks,' said Omer. 'He ain't all wrong. But he didn't mean to be nice by it.'

'One of them new uppity East Coast transplants,' added Smithwick.

'You aren't getting anything for $300 off of him,' said Gretchen.

Omer felt a wave of defeat wash over him. He understood that the world he dreamed of was a very different sort of place than the reality he could afford.

'Suppose I could help,' she continued.

'We listening,' replied Smithwick.

'You need help in putting that hot rod together,' she said. 'No offence, but I did see that when we looked over the frame in there. I've taken apart enough of those engines and cars that Omer here thinks you need to build.'

Omer nodded, grinned a little. He knew that she was right. He and Smithwick were more dreamers than doers. Smithwick appeared bothered by Gretchen's offer. 'Sounds good,' Omer said regardless.

'You two do need an engine,' replied Gretchen. Her attention was focused on Smithwick.

Smithwick rattled the ice in his cup. Across the street two men laughed loudly from inside Mike's garage. A door slammed shut and a cold grey Acura pulled out, backed down the paved driveway and honked three chipper beeps before turning onto the road and driving away under the train overpass. What sounded like jazz floated out from the direction of the garage.

'She's right you know,' said Omer.

'Shit,' replied Smithwick, 'I know.' He pulled out his pack of blue American Spirits. Rummaged through his pocket and pulled out the small round container for his hash. Mike stepped out of his garage, looked across the road at them, then walked across his parking lot towards a black Mercedes. Smithwick dipped his cigarette in the hash oil inside. He lit the cigarette, took two hard pulls and watched as Mike drove the Mercedes into the garage. 'Still up to you two to get the engine. But, yeah, we need some help.'

———————————

Omer didn't think of Jenny Geffler that often anymore. He'd been married long enough to know that his marriage to the former Miss Trina Oblack had made him into the man he was. However, on this particularly muggy, hot morning at the Elletsville Junkyard, he thought of Jenny. It was crawling on towards noon, and he and Gretchen were scavanging the most recent arrivals to the junkyard for wires, bearings and other car parts. This time, rather than following a scribbled list from Smithwick, Gretchen was calling out parts they should look for as they approached individual wrecks. When they reached the remains of a decade-old Passat, Gretchen bent over and, in her tight, cut-off jean shorts, he saw Jenny Geffler's ass again.

Saw her like it was the 1988 Monroe County Fair on a hazy-dark Indiana evening in August, both of them teenagers in a John Cougar Mellencamp kind of way. Jenny bent over the hulk of a ruined Nissan that was going nowhere in the foreseeable future. 'An ass to make dinner plans with', as his Uncle Bill would say, and it was on full display. Jenny was easily the hottest girl at Bloomington South, and Omer had managed to convince her out on a couple of dates. He would consider the county fair the high-water mark of pretty much his entire life for one main reason: she had caught him staring at her ass in very similar jean shorts to the ones he was currently appreciating. When Jenny had turned around and smiled at him, invited him to touch it, he had felt for the first time in his life that he had made it in the world. A gorgeous woman had thought enough of Omer to allow him to fulfil one of his cherished fantasies. It had all gone to hell a few days later, but that moment had stuck with him.

'I know my ass is a work of art,' said Gretchen wryly, shattering his daydream. 'I roller derby. Great for the glutes. But you're married, and all this ogling is not becoming. Our working relationship might suffer.' She stood up with a fistful of wires, waved them playful-like.

'Makes you feel better, it wasn't actually you.' He pulled the wires out of her hand and tossed them into a large bag he was carrying. It was full of their part-scrounging victories. 'You reminded me of someone,' he stated nonchalantly.

Gretchen was momentarily perplexed before letting out a startled laugh. 'Omer, you are one particular kind of man.' She steered them towards another car, a Hyundai wrecker from a city in love with road salt. 'I remind you of someone, huh? Care to elaborate?'

'Not really,' Omer said with a shrug. He had heard that description applied to him before. He gathered it came from the fact that he had rarely taken to brash—or even overtly visible—displays of emotion. 'High school ain't something you shake easy.'

'No shit.' Gretchen forced up the hood of the car. Something popped in the hinges, and slid off to the side opposite to them. 'Damn, it looks almost new in there.' She stooped over again, poking around intermittently through a pile of rocker panels, door frames and lift-gates.

'It does look pretty good for a wrecker,' said Omer. 'Even got some shine to it.'

'Your embarrassing display of wandering eyes got me thinking,' said Gretchen. 'Just seeing this'—she slapped her own ass—'had you drooling, probably thinking about your high school sweetheart's adolescent behind. Bet that little trip down memory lane made your day, too. So, thinking along those lines, a little switcheroo with this baby'—she patted the pristine Hyundai engine—'might be the answer to our problems.'

Gretchen was clearly flattered and amused by Omer's gawking, and he didn't want to ruin her pleasure by admitting his gaze frequently wandered. The college girls around town, transient as crows in the fall, generally considered him to be creepy even from afar, someone to flee. Gretchen was nothing like them in spirit and bore little resemblance to them in form. 'Not sure what you're getting at,' he said.

'Course not,' Gretchen said. She was visibly exasperated with Omer's denseness. He recognized it from Trina. 'Smithwick and you don't like that Mike guy across the street?'

'Might not describe our feelings perfectly,' replied Omer, 'but sure.'

'He works on Hondas, right?' asked Gretchen.

'You're not thinking of robbing him, are you?' Omer was neither alarmed nor amused by her implication.

'It's not robbing him. It's more of a … trade,' she said. She pointed at an old Dodge Neon engine resting on some blocks nearby.

'But that don't work,' Omer replied.

'That don't matter,' she answered. 'He's a mechanic. He'll get it to work well enough.'

'He might notice,' Omer said. He was still working out the proper response to this.

'It's gonna take him time.' Gretchen pulled at the engine, ferreting out the weight of it all, perhaps the size. 'Looks about the right size to pull an easy switch on him. Replace some stickers or at least peel off the old ones and he might never figure it out. If he's a good mechanic, he might even fool himself into thinking it's worth using. And besides, what are the chances he thinks of you two if he notices someone stole his engine?'

'Well he ain't really said much to us,' said Omer. 'He just glares at us from across the street like we're bringing down his business just by sitting on paint buckets in the driveway.' He considered the way the breeze whipped around a loose piece of blue vinyl poking up from a nearby pile.

'I'll do the swap,' she said. 'For, like, two hundred. Done it a good many times. I'd call it an easy job. Two hundred, even.'

Omer held his gaze on the vinyl. He was certain that it was from a seat, maybe even a shred of a belt. It continued to flicker back and forth in the wind. The silence that followed was awkward as he thought about the need to pay her. The idea was hers and the risk was also hers, but they were supposed to be working together as a team. As far as Omer could tell from the last few days, Gretchen had no real job, but she drove a pretty nice Dodge truck and had big-city clothes and tastes, more so than he and Smithwick. By all measures, two hundred seemed fair enough—less than he was willing to pay, even. He stared at her uncomfortably. 'Yeah,' he said eventually. 'We should do that.'

'What you figure Bird is running this year?' inquired Smithwick. He and Omer were sitting by the firepit waiting for Gretchen to arrive from Indy with the engine. She'd done the swap the previous night, with help from her own accomplices, well after Mike had closed for the day, leaving the neighbourhood to the tree frogs and the rednecks. She arrived as Mike was packing up shop for the night, pulling up the street before backing easily down the earthen divot of a driveway to the work garage. She flooded Mike's place with her high beams before putting the truck in park and hopping out.

'Twenty-six days, boys,' she hollered across the lawn. 'Twenty-six days to get this car running.' The race was a little over a month away and they needed time to fine tune and get the driving thing down.

'Heard Cummins threw him an experimental,' said Omer. He had heard the rumour during a call-in show on Bedford Community TV. He had taken to watching the channel a great deal lately on account of them airing Mexican wrestling and replays of the short-track races from up in Indy. The local sports call-in show had followed it and provided just enough entertainment for him to stay awake at least until it ended.

'Bedford awaits!' Gretchen yelled and walked into the garage.

'That is plenty soon,' Smithwick said. He and Omer got up and followed Gretchen into the garage. She had already pulled the latches off the hood and was forcing the metal up. Omer immediately grabbed the other end and helped her ease the hood off.

'The missus is okay with you out late?' joked Gretchen.

'Took her and the kids to the library,' said Omer. 'They got their movies and are watching them with Grannie.'

'His grandma lives down the street,' Smithwick added, 'which is why he comes around so much.'

'Yep,' said Omer. 'My lady takes care of her and the boys. Granny's house is bigger than ours.'

'Aren't you two just the perfect small town Indiana neighbourhood boys.' She retrieved the lift crane and got them to help her remove the engine from the bed of her truck. The lights shut off across the street and Mike pulled his bronze Audi out of his garage. He hesitated for a moment and watched them as they hoisted the engine into the air then dragged it into the garage bay.

'You seen that?' asked Omer. 'He still staring us down.'

'You should be happy he watched us,' said Gretchen. 'He should be wondering what we're doing.'

'I know what Omer is saying, though,' Smithwick said. 'That guy is just another wannabe East Coast rich guy. Been selling himself to the university-imported "intellectuals" for so long he's got to thinking that he's all that much better than us.' Smithwick used air quotes around the word intellectuals for necessary emphasis.

'Lot of Bloomington's gotten like that,' Omer added.

'What is it that you want from this race?' she asked. The tone of her voice signalled her intent to channel the men's simmering anger.

'Same thing as most men,' said Smithwick. 'Another crack at the type of renown working for a living don't get you.'

'And the ten-thousand-dollar purse,' Omer added matter-of-factly.

'I like the sound of that,' answered Gretchen. 'Even when it's split three ways.'

'Gotta beat Larry Bird too,' said Smithwick.

'Damn right,' said Omer. He nodded his head emphatically. 'Biggest East Coast sellout. Boston Celtics are pretty damned far from his Indiana State Sycamore roots.'

Gretchen paused. She was lining up the engine to the frame. She shook her head ever so slightly before she spoke. 'You two really hate that guy.'

'Everyone knows he enters the race every year just to remind guys like us who gets all the cake,' said Omer.

'Ain't no one talk about Bird's shit up in Indy,' added Smithwick. He had detected Gretchen's cynicism about Bird being at all involved in the race. 'It's all about Larry's legend up there. Like he ain't ever done something for even the Pacers. What does the city care if Larry Bird comes down here and shit-kicks some poor locals in a county fair race?'

'Not much,' offered Gretchen. 'Which is why I don't exactly believe you about Larry Bird. No way a guy as rich and old as him is going to spend a minute down here on an amateur county race. It'd be nice to actually win the race … and the money.' Omer and

Smithwick agreed with her on the second count by issuing confident ummhmmms that gave the impression it didn't really matter what she believed or didn't.

The three of them worked well into the night, wiring the engine into the frame and attempting to find balance and precision in what was a collage of all the things they couldn't afford.

Three weeks later autumn had turned on an unexpected heat that left Omer daydreaming about carefree teenage summers and spending as much time as he could away from Trina and the boys. Mostly he watched old stock car races on Gretchen's phone while she and Smithwick worked on the hot rod.

They christened the car the Rosewater after Grannie's last name. Gretchen had proclaimed that it had a ring to it that would make the geezers believe some old-monied family had come up with the backing for the car.

On the Thursday before the Bedford rally, the three of them tested the Rosewater in the parking lot of the abandoned Kmart on the outskirts of town.

At completion, the Rosewater sported a slate-grey body, shaped like something between early 1990s Honda Accord and a Ricardo Montalban Chrysler boat. A fire-breathing Corgi was painted on its hood—bug-eyed, as if in mid-strike—as a homage to Smithwick's dog, and to give it a sense of fierceness. The orange, red and yellow flames were more 1980s anime than real. She was partially street legal in that she posed little threat to real sports cars in form; the majority of her functionality was hidden by the mundane realities of everyday driving.

Omer piloted the car between the imaginary barriers of fading parking lot lines. Trina and the boys sat with Smithwick and Gretchen, watching from a boulevard between the shuttered store and the bulk of the lot as he made faster and faster circles, pushing both himself and the Rosewater to the limits until they reached that fine line that separated the everyday from the legendary. About five minutes later, Trina and the kids tired of watching him doing his burn outs and imaginary laps. They deserted him for the Hardee's across the street.

After his sixteenth go around, he pulled over beside Gretchen and Smithwick. He emerged from the car, sweat-drenched and full of the adrenaline he hadn't experienced since his football days. 'That look good?' he asked, partially rhetorically, as he sat down on the curb beneath a desiccated wisp of a pear tree. 'It felt good.'

'Looking good in a car is one thing,' answered Gretchen. 'Winning a race is something else.' She approached the Rosewater, popped the hood, lifted it and began poking around the engine.

'No leaks?' asked Smithwick.

'Clean,' she replied.

'Yeah, but did I look like a real driver out there?' Omer persisted.

'You looked fine, man,' answered Smithwick. 'You are the only driver we have, so you *are* a real driver.'

'How did the car feel?' asked Gretchen.

Omer could think of little else but how the Rosewater felt, how the machine moved and followed his whims and movements. He considered his car, a 2002 Dodge Caravan, the way it felt like time passing as he shuffled between work and Grannie's and school and home. He looked down at his still-gloved hands, and he could feel in them a light buzzing. Time had not simply been passing in the Rosewater. Omer had felt alive, as if he had been chasing prey just beyond his grasp. The buzzing was a reminder that he had been something completely different from that which he was each and every day. He and the Rosewater had been connected in ways he had never before experienced. It jumped and twitched with his every move and thought. He said nothing. He looked into Gretchen's dirty-grey eyes and smiled so widely that his mustache curled upward at the ends.

Race day at the Bedford County Fairgrounds had carried forward the same dry yet thick heat that had pervaded the final week or so of the rapidly closing season. Omer had spent much of the afternoon lounging on a bank of hay bales by the racecar parking area. He had given Trina and the kids the lion's share of a week's salary to spend on rides, food and the attractions of the midway. They had been gone for the better part of two hours, and he was far from upset about their absence. Smithwick and Gretchen were fussing over the Rosewater a few feet away. Omer for the most part ignored them, watched the younger moms and daughters stroll by.

He felt no nervousness going into what would be his first race. Over the past few days behind the wheel of the Rosewater, he had felt more at home, more in control, more emotional than he had in as long as he could remember. This was what the Lord Almighty had placed Omer Counce on Earth to do. Omer had just now found his calling. He simply knew that his life centred on driving a car as fast as he could. When he sat in the seat of the Rosewater to take the Bedford Fairgrounds dirt short-track at highway-plus speed, it would be his first but very far from his last time behind the wheel of a performance car.

Omer saw him then, walking through the quiet and tense centre of the mechanic's pit. Larry Bird was tall and lanky like a Sesame Street morning, standing beside his oldest boy. Outside of his height and horrible beak of a nose, Bird looked like any other past-middle-aged Southern Indiana man. Blue jeans, runners and a polo shirt said he cared little for his image among these people. Omer watched him walk up to a group of men working on a blue-and-gold car at the far end. He recognized their mechanic neighbour after a few short seconds. Mike was working on the car with Bird's crew. Omer scrambled to his feet, hustled over to Gretchen, Smithwick and the Rosewater as quickly and quietly as he could manage.

'Son-of-a-bitch Bird is here,' he muttered while he tugged on the back of Smithwick's shirt.

'No way,' replied Gretchen. She swung around before Smithwick did, wildly scanning the pit and its crews. 'Where?' She halted mid-question, without doubt spying the awkward-looking tall man a good distance away. 'You two weren't just bullshitting.'

'No news in that,' replied Smithwick.

'That's not it,' said Omer. 'The uppity bastard Mike is working for him.'

'Wait, what?' snapped Gretchen. She was frantically searching for Mike amongst the distance car crew.

'Figures,' answered Smithwick. He nonchalantly turned back to his work on the Rosewater. Omer could tell he was pissed, not alarmed, and that the anger would rise slow like flood waters.

'Guys.' Gretchen pulled Omer's arm to draw his attention. 'That car of theirs look familiar?'

Omer squinted, stared hard at the car. Couldn't make anything special out of it. 'Nope,' he said. Smithwick did not look up from the Rosewater.

'That's what's left of the Accord we swapped the engine out of,' she pronounced.

Omer was slack jawed at the thought. 'They running the car on that busted up old thing?'

Gretchen laughed in response. 'Depends if Mike was a good enough mechanic to put it back together.'

The car Bird's crew was working on revved up loud enough for the three to hear it.

'Guess so,' said Smithwick. 'Doesn't sound too frightening.'

Omer considered the engine their key to the entire competition and felt no less confident than he did before. Smithwick and Gretchen wanted the win. Omer needed to drive. For a moment he thought of himself as a butterfly emerging from a cocoon, but then, he never cared for bugs. Maybe he was more like an alligator hatching from an egg: a predator erupting into the world, ready to strike. For Omer, all that mattered was that he fed on what truly nourished him before moving on to the next thing. The thing that would free him, put him back on the path to becoming the man he knew instinctively that he needed to be. Gretchen and Smithwick could keep the money. Omer simply needed the glory, the spotlight shining upon him. 'I got this,' he declared to his teammates. He returned his attention to Smithwick. 'How long we got?'

Smithwick checked his cellphone. 'About twenty minutes,' he said.

Omer nodded. He said nothing and wandered away to the washrooms, flexing his hands, trying to recapture that tingling feeling he had felt in the parking lot of that vacant Kmart. The tingle returned after he did his business and gave his hands a quick cold-water wash. By the time he returned to the Rosewater, Omer could almost feel the bulk of the steering wheel beneath his fingers and against his palms. There was a growing rumble at the base of his neck, one that grew in its intensity by the moment.

Under the lights of the Bedford Fairgrounds short track, Omer sat loose limbed in the driver's seat of the Rosewater. He had been placed in the fourth pair from the front alongside a guy from Vincennes in a remodelled Ford Focus. He gave the guy, pork-fed chubby and clean-shaven, the customary nod that he often bestowed on like-minded but younger men when he came across them. The man glared back nervously then offered a half-smile. Omer turned his attention forward, first to the bumpers of the two cars before him (both standard-looking sedans he guessed to be GM body types) then beyond them to the first row of cars. He could make out the rear of Bird's team's car, the blue and gold obvious even through two windshields and two back windows between them. Omer knew he would catch them.

It was then that he noticed the flag girl. She was high above the cars in a Bedford Fire Department cherry picker bucket, flag still by her side. She was about eighteen, with long, straight, dark hair and bare legs that made Omer forget about the rest of her. He wasn't so much smitten with her look as he was impressed. Over the rising revving of the engines around him, he couldn't hear her, but he could make out her giggles through the shuffle of her movements. She had much more optimistic jitters than the drivers around him. He watched her with an intensity that lasted for what was surely too long, and towards the end, she stood up straight, completely earnest and dropped the flag in frantic sweeps across a blacktop sky.

Omer shifted the Rosewater into gear and followed the slow-building explosion of speed and volume as the field of hot rods settled into formation. The moments passed with ever-increasing speed in a shuffle of cars and dirt and near misses.

Bedford Country Fairground's mechanical lights made the air itself look as if it were burning back the phosphorescent lights from above. The growl of the engines and the blankness of continual yellowish light made Omer feel as if he were in a trance—the sort of trance that, according to Grannie, the reverend said was gifted to all men and women of the Lord. Omer made out Larry Bird's car a few rows ahead of him, and he swore he could feel the Rosewater grumble a little, like the working folk ready to hit back at their blowhard boss. Omer followed the movements of the car. His vision was its vision, gaze resting steadfastly forward, past each one of the cars before them, on the small glimpses of a wide-open all-American road. Everything slid around Omer in slow motion. Inch by inch, the Rosewater gained on the cars ahead.

At the midway point of the twenty-fifth lap, the Rosewater had almost caught up to Bird's car. While the thirty-three painted on the trunk was far from gaudy it still bothered Omer.

He could see Bird's car in the lead. The Rosewater was now only a single car's length away from him. The last portion of the race opened up just beyond. Omer understood that the time had arrived for him to make his moves, break past the number thirty-three car and gain the open road before them all. He took a few half-laps in loose swings, sizing up how to fit between the cars. One was a rebuild of a 1980s Chevy Cavalier done by a guy who liked barbeques. The other was a paint-slopped camo-green bean of a car that looked built of old riding lawnmowers and rusted K-cars. As Omer began to put more weight on the gas, he noticed the first jet-stream wisp of white jut out from Bird's car. In less than an eighth of a mile, the wisp exploded into a cloud, and Omer had the good sense to point the Rosewater to the outside left and power through. With the growl of an old barn cat, the Rosewater punched through the dense cloud of blown-engine steam to the open track before him, and burst past the outstretched checkered flag.

Omer let the momentum carry him. At once, he let all thoughts escape him. He had won the Bedford IU Credit Union Motorsports Rally. He had done what every Southern Indiana Hoosier believed impossible: he had bested Larry Bird. And yet the crowd did not matter. The money did not matter. The adoration of Smithwick and Gretchen for his crackpot driving; the possibility that Trina might stop yelling at him; the off chance that just one of his sons might respect him enough to listen to his demands—none of it mattered. What mattered was the feeling of the car beneath him, the steady mechanic vibration of the engine through his fingertips. Omer felt alive, born into the bright, bathing warmth of the unseasonably warm night. He followed that feeling, decelerated the Rosewater enough to safely navigate it off the track through the wide-open space reserved for emergency vehicles. He pushed through; the odd straggler from the fair looked back at him, perplexed, before sliding aside. The Rosewater eased its way through the gravel and dirt of the lot until she kicked up like a bison escaping the hatchet man and burst onto 37 South. The Rosewater gained speed as Omer glided to the places he knew he had to be.

BREAKING RIGHT

'My favourite ball is the knuckler. I hold the ball tight against the knuckles of my pitching hand and throw it with every ounce of speed I can put behind it. When it's breaking right, it swoops down a good deal like a curve, only faster and with a sharper break. I don't believe any batter in uniform likes to face a good knuckle ball when it's sweeping in with a lot of zip and breaking right.'
—Jesse Haines, in an interview for the May 1928 issue of *Baseball Magazine*

Although she had never been there, could never have been there, Nadine pictures that 1924 night in St. Louis as if it marked the birth of the entire world. Philip had told the tale often enough; he had recited it before every ball game she ever followed him to, almost always in the company their other constant companion, Erin. The tale was a glimmer from his Grandfather Leskew's early days working alongside the nation's pastime. Grandfather Leskew had run the scoreboard for Sportsman's Park and had witnessed it all as if it were a gospel unfolding. He passed down the Word to Philip's father, who passed it down to Philip, who told it to Nadine, until the story had lodged itself firmly into her memories of Philip and Louisville, and until it had managed to manifest itself even in the fabric of the life she had tried to build away from them.

On that particular day, it is a broadcast from a nearby fisherman's radio that walks her through a Mariners's at-bat. Nadine is at the docks in downtown Newport, looking out into Oregon's Pacific Ocean. She watches as a fog bank drifts past the Yaquina Bay Bridge in the distance. She is taken by how the soft, white, weightless body of cloud wraps itself around the cold metal of the bridge, the way that wisp-like manifestations of creation soften the hard edges of reality. Figgins fans on a breaker down and in, retiring the side. She hears in these nearby echoes the mythological showdown of Jesse Haines and Casey Stengel that she can't shake.

Afternoon opens humid and heavy, as if the great Mississippi spread itself out and into the air and over the shores and around the hard body of St. Louis. Daylight falls through the brown haze of midwestern America. Sweet-tea coloured, the light fans through the grass-like sway of the crowd at Sportsman's Park. Jesse Haines is on the mound in the ninth and without a single base hit through their nine-man order.

The Boston Braves send up Casey Stengel to face Haines. Haines is known for his knuckleball, a pitch that traces its ancestry through its illegal counterpart, the spitball. The crowd maintains an unsteady murmur, ready to erupt in a roar of delight—or a collective groan all-too-familiar to those gathered in the stands. This is the closest to a no-hitter a Cardinals pitcher has ever come. Twenty-six up, twenty-six down, one to go. Casey Stengel, an outfielder who earned fame for his heroics in the World Series the previous year, takes two balls in the dirt and fouls off three, driving Haines's pitch count up to 130. Haines is exhausted. Between the heat and the teeth-grinding force he pushes every throw—fastball, curve, knuckle, knuckle, fastball—his arm drops loose like a wild grapevine to hover just above the copper-coloured dirt of the mound.

Fans halfway up the third-baseline grandstands can see from Haines's expression that he knows he needs to make this one last pitch. He has to make it because his runs against average is way high at a notch above five a game. He has to make it because, despite the fact that he won twenty games last year, he has crawled out to just four wins thus far this season. Haines knows it as well as any Cardinals-loving fan. The Cardinals's catcher, Mike Gonzalez, senses it too, drops the sign for Haines to throw the new pitch. So, Haines tosses the knuckleball, releasing it with a half-limp arm and a groan you could hear across the river in Illinois. The ball explodes from his fingertips, follows a high arc through the ninety feet to the plate, but slows and appears to hang in the upper batter's box, in the sweet spot that batters usually ride to the gaps between fielders. Stengel swings, pulling the bat off his shoulder and kicking his leg up from the dirt. But the ball breaks, slightly downward and right, and Stengel's bat glances over the top of the ball and drives it into the grass between the plate and the pitching mound. The humid air clings to the grass and holds the ball to two short hops to Haines's feet. Stengel is about a third of the way down the first-base line by the time Haines picks up the ball and shuttles it over to first base, ending the game.

It was the only no-hitter any Leskew ever saw in person. Nadine remembers Philip recounting that story. She can hear his voice in her head, how it pulls that memory from roots dug into the rich, dark soil of the Ohio River Valley. The story was as much part of him as was the land, the air, the ground he called home, a home that defined the entirety of Nadine's life just a few years ago. She heads to the house her father shares with his lover. She moves inland and is haunted by things she believed she left behind.

———————

It has been a little over a year since the last time Nadine has sat atop the fossil beds that stretch westward from the Falls of the Ohio. She is sitting on one of the shale outcroppings. A haze extends upward from where the nearby water crumples into itself. The violent rumble pushes up a slight whiteness that dulls the edges of distant Louisville's skyline. Nadine leans back against the rock behind her and stretches her mud-splotched legs outward atop the shadow-patched rock. Her skin is as pale as she could ever recall it being in all the time she spent along these riverbanks, pale like the limestone fossil beds meeting the muddy body of the river. The Crock-Pot heat that simmers along the intersection of the lower Midwest and the South drags down on Nadine's thick mess of brown hair, and she wants nothing more than to lift the limp strands off her neck. She wants to, but doesn't, because Nadine can discern in her body the bone-deep exhaustion born of an hour-long fight with the river. A tired-looking spincast rod lies unused beside her.

'He's still at it, huh?' Erin says. Erin is a tall, wide-hipped and thin-faced redhead. She hands Nadine a plastic water bottle. Nadine holds her arm then her hand out in a little-kid-gimme kind of way, then drops both limply beside her once the bottle meets the fleshy part of her palm.

Nadine nods. 'Relentless,' she says. 'It's like he's still seventeen and it's not hotter than all hell out here.' Erin laughs and leans against a nearby tree. Nadine watches as the sharp-edged white crests of the water settle into determined rolling lumps. 'I've always been pretty terrible at this.' Nadine shakes the fishing rod beside her.

'Oregon might be making you a little soft,' says Erin.

'The heat, you mean.'

'Couple of seasons outside Louisville and you already start forgetting things.'

Nadine pulls her hair back, hoping that it will lift some of the humid weight from her shoulders. It doesn't. Her arms are exhausted. She drops them to her sides again. Nadine can just make out the small figure that is Philip standing in front of the fast-falling water. He is further up the shore. She is certain she can make out his movements against the constant collapse of the river over the spillway.

Philip is wading out into the edges of the more turbulent water. Shirtless, sun-bronzed and careless, he pushes into the water like a cowboy certain the horse beneath him will not buck. He is alone. The crash of water is too much to holler over. It's numbing in its ever-presence. The smell of Indiana as it meets Kentucky is that of the breath of a man in the morning. The scent is heavy and full of the moisture of tar-filled lungs, putrid and fresh with the richness of river-fed earth. Philip is trying to hit the legendary run of channel cats, and he's throwing the fishing line as if his knuckles are pressed against the hard-woven skin of a baseball. And the line, the line is swooping down a good deal like a curve and breaking from its path sharp and quick. At the waterline there is no breeze; none there and none where Nadine is standing.

Nadine feels this stagnation, feels it on the rocks above the less violent portion of the Ohio. Droplets fall like soot. The air is tainted with the smell of burnt wood—maybe sycamore, maybe oak. She is reclining against the coolness of the rock behind her and she wants to listen to Philip, wants to work with the heat, to move with its passing ripples. Maybe at one time she could have worked with it. That was before, though, and right now places her in heat-induced exhaustion. Nadine's life is now a world away, along the distant Pacific Ocean. This moment is akin to a memory being revisited. She has been here a thousand times, with the same people doing the same thing. But she is an observer now.

Erin crouches down beside her. 'He might not seem so happy,' says Erin, 'but he is. He's glad you're back.' Erin is a year and a bit younger than Nadine and Philip. They had grown up together, all of them attending New Albany High School. Erin had played varsity basketball, Philip baseball. Nadine watched. They had been close friends since the days a bike ride to the convenience store felt like the equivalent of the Lewis and Clark expedition. They had all remained in New Albany through college and the world after. All of them except Nadine.

'It feels good to be back,' says Nadine. And she is being truthful because she wishes the rock that she is sitting atop and the August heat that is smothering her would still feel as comfortable and ordinary as they did the day she left. They don't, but she still wants to pretend that everything is as it should be, or more appropriately, as it was months ago. A few days back in Kentuckiana and still it hadn't all fallen back into the places it should have. 'My mom's happy to have me around again. She still can't exactly figure out why I left.'

'Things working out in Oregon?' asks Erin. 'Is it everything you figured?'

'Yes and no,' says Nadine. The career and the fresh start are everything that she had hoped they would be when she boarded that flight months ago. The rest is all about leaving home. She has learned that life after leaving home is a mixed bag—it's only a little bit like what you dreamed it would be and never like it was before. 'It's not like here, but it's good.' She's playing half-nostalgic, half-modest, as if she doesn't want to show up the friend she left behind.

'You don't sound convinced,' Erin says, seeing through her attempt at humility.

'Well,' says Nadine, 'an opportunity came up and I had to take it.' Nadine looks back towards the falls and sees that Philip is coming their way. In the channel above them, a heavily laden coal barge inches along atop the nearly flat surface of the water with a steady, distant metallic clicking. Right there, right then, Nadine wants to tell Erin, before Philip makes it back to them, that it has been hard since she left. She feels as if there is a fundamental incompatibility between her new world and the world she had to leave behind, as if the worlds could not coexist without one corrupting the other. Nadine looks up at Erin. Clumps of sweat-drenched tresses anchor the billow of sun-dried, humidity-frizzed hair from Erin's head. Erin nods and motions for the water bottle. Nadine hands it to her. 'Marriage can do horrible things to you,' she says out of nowhere.

Erin nods. Nadine is sure it is more out of understanding than agreement. Over the years Erin has often talked about marriage. She has talked about marriage like any good Catholic girl would. Marriage like Nadine's very good Catholic mother has always talked about. Talked about, but failed to hold together.

The mind is left with the truth that the world so often wishes not to handle. Nadine read this on the back of a pamphlet a group of Mormon boys handed her in the Portland International Airport. 'Would you please take one of our pamphlets?' She remembers their quiet smiles when she took hold of one and tried her damnedest to look as though she was deeply interested in the pamphlet's contents, all while walking away from them at full stride to avoid any follow-up chit-chat. 'Thank you,' she had mumbled.

The decision to move her whole life to the coast arose partially from her growing up and partially from her desire to avoid becoming the embodiment of all the mistakes her parents had made. The rest unfolded so quickly that the entire uprooting of her world was reduced to a solitary answer: career. She told no one why. Not even her father and his partner, Cordero.

The pamphlet startled her at first, its words cutting too close to the truth very few could avoid: that place and family determine one's arc through life. She had feared this truth, and that fear had thrown her on a plane and carried away from the world that consistently pushed her onto the terrifying path of becoming her mother. She was so self-convinced, in those early months, that her decision to move west was the only right decision. She walked past the baggage claim and through the taxi stand, then she shook off the pang of guilt and pushed the pamphlet into her suitcase. She forgot about it rather quickly once she took the airport shuttle to Newport, to the world that her father had created for himself and his partner, a world away from the one that Nadine had just left.

She told Philip and Erin and her mother that there was work to be had in Newport, a photojournalist position at a community newspaper. While it was true that she couldn't find work in her field in Kentuckiana, she knew it was little more than a convenient excuse for her departure.

She found that pamphlet again as she packed that same bag to head to that same airport. Slightly larger than an overnight bag, the bag was the only piece of decent-looking luggage she owned. Nadine worked hard to make her new life look good to those she had left behind, mostly through limited social media posts and the scant handful of calls to those back in Kentuckiana. They appeared to believe in her success, and had mostly asked about her newest assignments and how life with a gay couple was treating her. The last remark came from her mother, who was almost always pointed and passive aggressive in the way she referred to her ex-husband as 'that gay man' or 'him'. She found that pamphlet in the bottom of an outside pocket, and as she opened the small, crinkled, bluish pages, the words of her mother rang through her head. Would knowing the truth about why Nadine had left—fear of marriage and the subtle violences it could bring—change the cutting remarks her mother made about her father? Mothers were mothers after all, Nadine thought. Catholic mothers were supposed to excel in the art of forgiveness.

Nadine held the small pamphlet between her fingers as she sat on the edge of the twin bed Cordero had set up for her in the office of her father's new family's home. The smooth pages with their elegant grey font ignited an ember of doubt among the certainties that had brought her to Oregon. That ember lingered in the grey, late-summer afternoon of coastal Oregon. A few rooms over, she heard the light tapping melody of a jazz piano—maybe Art Tatum or Bud Powell, as those were Cordero's favourite albums—and the nearby hiss of leaves turning about in the wind. Her mother's attitude toward marriage was only part of the reason Nadine had had to leave.

———————————

They are still in their sweat-soaked clothes, and the dirt of the Ohio lines the edges of their fingernails. The jukebox at Miranda's Tavern starts into Dan Auerbach's 'My Last Mistake'. Four of Philip's work friends from the ballpark have joined them at the table. Nadine recognizes a few of them. The one with the roundish face, short red hair and the beginnings of a beard is paying her a large amount of attention. Erin is telling a story about a night at Miranda's from after Nadine's escape. Everyone is watching Erin except for Philip's friend, who is watching Nadine.

The sun has left a lingering heat that Nadine feels in her face. She wonders if it looks at all like she's blushing, ashamed for missing out on the moments that bind friends together. She holds the beer bottle between her fingertips. Miranda's is quickly becoming a fusion of past familiarity and future discomfort. Nadine laughs out of the side of her mouth, nervously.

'So, the guy stands up,' Erin says. '"Who needs the fucking Cardinals anyway," he shouts. And I swear, no word of lie here, you remember that old glass mirror on that wall over there?' The heads at the table turn to a blank space next to the Old Bardstown Bourbon sign. 'Whole danged thing just up and fell off the wall on his sweet lovin' ass.' The table erupts into laughter.

Nadine smiles widely. She forces it. She thinks that must have hurt the guy, wonders if there was blood involved. Philip is buckled over in mirth. One hand is on the table. The other, she notices, disappears below its lip, angling off towards Erin's leg.

She plays cool, making like she hadn't seen anything. They were never like that before, Erin and Philip. Erin had met Philip through Nadine. Nadine feels a growing self-consciousness in her. She feels angry-sick. She's fairly certain Red is staring at her again.

'Son of a bitch deserved it,' says Philip. He's still laughing.

'To get crumbled by a forty-pound mirror?' Nadine sneers. She wants to make Philip feel the way she does. She wants him to pull his hand off Erin's knee. Philip looks up, surprised, returns both hands to the table.

'No, no,' says Erin. 'It's all right. He was all right, I mean. You just had to be there.'

'Suppose so,' Nadine says. 'Too much sun, sorry.' With all of the table's eyes on her, she reaches for the one topic that she is sure will comfortably change the darkening direction of the conversation and draw attention away from herself. 'So are the Cardinals gonna do well this year?'

'Better than the Reds,' says Red. Everyone howls in merriment.

One of the men raises his beer glass in salute. 'To our Cardinals,' he proclaims. Glasses clink and Nadine follows through hesitantly, hammers back the beer with the rest of them.

'How is Oregon?' Red prods.

Nadine can't look at him. She picks at the label on the beer bottle. She pictures Erin and Philip making out somewhere in the half-light around the river, feels jealousy and anger welling up. 'The ocean is awesome, and no mosquitoes.'

'Where you at out there?' asks Red. At least she thinks it's Red.

'Newport, central coast.'

'Must be nice.'

'It is, thanks.'

'Keeping yourself busy with all the photography?' asks Erin. The tone of her voice is nearly a boast, something akin to 'look at my really cool artistic friend'. Then she worries that maybe Erin knows. Knows that Nadine is a fraud, working at coffee shop, taking a few pictures here and there, and poor. Maybe the hardness of the *k* is directed at her like a metal-tipped prod: 'You left us all and you have done nothing and now I have to take care of Philip.' Nadine feels what she is certain is Red's chair slide closer to her, just slightly.

'Yeah,' Nadine says, 'I keep pretty busy.' She thinks of the white noise of the ocean hitting the shore, the cool greyness of coastal Oregon. She hears but can't decipher the murmurs of the radio. She looks at the dirt beneath her fingernails, feels the crinkly moulding of sweat-soaked clothes to her body, and knows that she's wandered into the wrong life. She scans the faces around the table. She wants them to look older, at least Erin and Philip, but none of them seem to have aged a day since she had hopped a plane west. Nadine wonders how she looks to them, wonders what shadows they see reflected in her eyes.

Philip looks like the Philip she remembers: sun-cooked, thin but muscular, with an ever-present five o'clock shadow. She wonders how often he thinks about that night, about the vast differences between the two separate worlds they now inhabit. Philip seems to be waiting for her to do something, to provide some form of entertainment, perhaps. Nadine thinks he may be looking for glimpses of the girl who once sat beside him, cruising down the highway between Indy and Louisville.

Nadine follows the line of his shoulder down his arm to his fingers, which twitch awkwardly, uncertain with nothing in their grip. Her gaze lands on Erin. She jokes with one of Philip's friends—not Red, but one of the other more wallflowery ones. Yet her upper body seems to rest against the outermost edge of Philip's personal space.

'What's up?' Philip asks.

Nadine watches Philip fiddle with his pint glass. He looks tense, as if shielding himself against the weight of Nadine's expectation. His body language suggests a sustained shield against those expectations. In that, she knows, his looks differ from what lies beneath. There is something of the past alive in Philip, and he is holding it back. This isn't her Philip. Nadine feels like an intruder. She is still exhausted from the afternoon by the Ohio and lacks the cognitive strength to wade through the bottomless well of anger and self-pity and empty sadness inside of her.

'I should go,' she says, loud enough for the table to hear. But she looks at Erin as she says it. Everyone mutters nice things as Nadine stands up. No one protests her departure.

Nadine and Philip made the two-hour drive north to Indianapolis via Interstate 65. It was the middle of fall and the majority of trees were either brown with ripeness or nude from the wind. Philip was driving, as he had since they first started their day trips sometime in late high school. This time there was no Erin, no other random friends from work or school. Just Philip and Nadine. They had gone to Indy to see a Pomegranates show and were returning in the wee hours of the morning. The Stones's *Exile on Main St.* was playing, and Nadine relaxed in the fuzzed-out aftermath of a shared joint.

'Sweet Virginia' came on the stereo, and Nadine was mesmerized by the lazy, sweeping call of the guitar, the certainty of Mick's voice. Its rolling gentleness was akin to the nonchalance of a barge moving downriver from Cincinnati or Pittsburgh.

The raw, unfiltered energy of the garage rock show that they had seen made Nadine want to move through her world at a higher speed, to push against the constant familiar. The feeling, simmering in the background for some time, had boiled over as a result of transit and music. In truth, her restlessness was a reaction to the mundanity of the everyday, the familiar, the way Philip teased and tantalized but almost never touched her. A tidal wave of resolve arose in her; the weed and the Stones music acted as rip currents sliding beneath the surface, carrying her away from her small, confined little life and out to sea.

'You ever get that feeling that sometimes we all just settle?' Nadine said. The clarity of the Stones broke under her words just as soon as they were uttered.

'Settle?' Philip asked.

'Yeah, kind of like, we all get comfortable doing one thing, like the world around us is set and it's all we could ever want. But really there is something that we're missing.'

'The what-if?'

'Yeah,' said Nadine. 'The what-if.' She thought about her father. She wondered if he was any happier with his new life. Her mother was very adamant that he wasn't—'Why else would he have disappeared out to Oregon?' Then again, Nadine wasn't exactly sure when or how the world of her childhood had changed for him. He just hadn't come back, *wouldn't* come back. Her mother had kept his last name, refused to sign the divorce papers.

'The grass is always greener,' said Philip.

'Is anything really that simple?' Nadine replied.

Philip nodded and went silent long enough for 'Sweet Virginia' to end. They passed Columbus and were almost halfway to New Albany. They drifted past reflective highway signs, light-flooded billboards and the off-road glare of gas stations and fast-food joints. Nadine reached over and searched for Philip's arm but found his knee with her open palm instead.

It was the first time that she remembered touching him. They had danced through some awkward moments over the years, had conversations about her boyfriends, his girlfriends. On the rarest occasions they would pass each other with the scrounged-up accessories that were these temporary partners. In all those years of knowing each other, they had never actually managed to touch. No hugs, handshakes, taps on the shoulder. Nothing. Maybe it was out of fear. Or maybe it was a recognition that whatever it was they had could, perhaps would, be lost if the start-stop ebb and flow of a physical relationship swept them past platonic friendship.

Philip said nothing. He pulled the car over at the next turnoff and they made love for their first and only time.

They made love in the shadows near a private woodlot. Afterwards, Nadine thought they should have planned it better, thought it out more. They moved by instinct. It was cold and humid and the night was full of long blue shadows that draped off the darkness around the trees. It was the kind of sex that should have happened long ago. It left her ears ringing with the angular, clinical sound of the word 'intercourse' and the stinging guilt of crossing a line that never should have been crossed. When it was done, they sat stiffly in the back seat and smoked the last of the weed. Rather than speak, Philip and Nadine sat and looked out over the hills and patchwork farmland of Southern Indiana.

She was in her mother's kitchen, a night after she had first talked to her father and Cordero about going out to Oregon for a visit. Nadine held one of her photos, framed its edges with her outstretched fingers and thumbs. A tug pushed a barge through the upper locks of the Falls of the Ohio. Heavy white ridges of churned-up river water stretched behind the tug as it powered against the current. The early colours of fall had begun to punctuate some of the lines of trees extending up from the water. The water reminded her of photos she had taken of Philip as he hit the catfish run. She rummaged through a stack of manila envelopes, pulling a sleeve of prints and a data stick from the middle of a nearby pile.

Nadine and Philip hadn't exchanged so much as a text message since their trip to Indy. The lack of communication between them was exceedingly rare. First the avoidance was of necessity—she needed to step back, keep her distance, figure out what had happened and how, and what it might mean. Then it was out of desire—not for Philip, if she was honest, but for Philip to desire her, to reach out first. Then it was anger—anger over the uncertainly and loss of control she felt. It was a reality that Nadine was comfortable with, if only because distance from the event had made her realize that she was not in love with Philip in the way she wanted to be. She had been in love with the idea of change, of addressing some of the what-ifs in her life, of shaking up that unattainable reality that Louisville and New Albany had become for her.

She remembered Philip telling her that throwing a cast was like throwing a pitch. He explained it on the shore as he tried to teach her about throwing a line. He explained it again during the warm-ups at Louisville Slugger Field before the teams took the field. It was about angles, Philip would say. Pitching was about throwing near the target. Like fishing, it was about luring in the batter with what they wanted, then denying them at the last second. You were constantly aiming ahead of the invisible line you were trying to hit. A strong, right-breaking pitch, just like the one Haines had thrown to finish off Stengel, was a thing of absolute beauty. It was the cast that every Leskew or fisherman or pitcher longed to throw in his lifetime. That pitch—the precision and artistry that went into the motions behind it—was the framework upon which to build multiple lifetimes. Nadine thought about Philip's words, about the impossible memory of that impossible moment with that impossible man who lived the better part of a century before them.

The lines and light in the photo were as warming as a nostalgic dream and distant as the golden era of baseball. It was taken months before Indy, before her world had changed, suddenly and sharply. Nadine knew at once that the world of those photos was gone, that that *Philip* was gone, consumed and changed by the roadside shadows that night on the way home from Indy. It was clear to Nadine that she had to leave Louisville, to discover who she was outside of the familiar rivers and stadiums and friendships and the only home she'd ever known. But her mother was still reeling from her husband's departure to Oregon some three years ago. Her mother was the type of Catholic woman who had denied the divorce and remained convinced that eventually her husband would realize his sinful ways and return home, asking for forgiveness.

Nadine speculated that she, herself, was more like her father than she'd ever realized. Had he felt trapped in Louisville, too? Had he been pierced by the barbs of what-ifs until they overwhelmed him, popped the comfortable little bubble of the world he had come to inhabit?

And what about Philip? Their relationship would have to change, or they, too, would be haunted by what-ifs. His world was this old version of New Albany: fighting channel catfish, baseball and cold beers at Miranda's. It was the world they enjoyed together, albeit separately. It was the world that Nadine still wanted to be hers and hers alone. Sharing, she had learned from the way her parents had treated each other, had a way of ending in utter, miserable catastrophe. The only safety that prevented her following that same path led her out west, to Oregon with her father. When he had called a few hours before, she had agreed to visit around New Year's.

Nadine avoided Philip and Erin for almost two weeks. She tried to avoid her mother, but shared meals and the requisite weekly trip to mass ruined that possibility. Nadine spent hours by the riverfront photographing the numerous bridges dotting the shore and capturing the way the light played off the old industrial buildings. The world went numb. Every building, tree, rock and waterline had an unfamiliar hollow edge to it. Erin called and Nadine chalked up the quiet terseness in her own voice to letters she had received from her dad.

Philip showed up at her mother's house the week before Christmas. He knocked at the door just as the last heavy traces of sun disappeared into night.

'Hey,' Nadine said.

Philip followed her into the kitchen. Photos were scattered and bundled into piles on the table. Atop them lay a notepad that Nadine was using to catalogue their individual defects. The more she examined them, the more defects she found, until the photos came to depict a fallen world.

Nadine positioned the breakfast bar between them. 'How are things?' As she looked at his very tired eyes, Nadine felt a sudden deep compassion for the man before her. The complaint was somewhat close to pity, but not quite there. 'Howlin' Wolf' was playing on a radio in the other room. She knew she didn't look half as rough as he did.

'Work's been slow. The off-season, you know. You?'

Nadine stood beside the stool, leafed open another page of the notepad. 'Busy,' she said, 'I really got into a project.' Nadine held up a night shot of the Clark Memorial Bridge. The colours were off, a little too bluish for her. Outside the trees shook in a passing wind, the branches creaking as they bent.

'Pretty cool,' Philip said, lower lip protruding slightly.

'I'm heading out to Oregon to visit my dad for New Year's,' Nadine said. 'I'm really hoping to give him and Cordero a few nice hangable photos for their place.'

'Cordero?' asked Philip.

'He's my father's partner,' she said. 'He's from out there. He's a great guy.'

'Your mom know about him?'

'I'm pretty sure she does. But she doesn't say much. How can she, right?' Nadine laughed.

'Sorry I didn't call,' Philip blurted out. Nadine felt the sting of something close to pride. She had begun to think less and less about Philip over the last week. Now she was annoyed by the notion that he thought her world centred on him. She could have called him, too. She was as much at fault as he was.

'Why?' she answered with a tenderness that surprised her. 'I could have. No need to feel bad. We both got occupied. I just haven't had the kind of time I wanted to have.'

'You talked to Erin?' Philip asked. He leaned against the counter.

'Here and there,' she said. 'Like I said, I've been working through these photos for my dad. You know if I get a couple recognized I could maybe land something better than a clerical job at the church.'

'Maybe,' said Philip. He had backed up and was leaning against the fridge. 'We've been distant since the Pomegranates show.' Nadine sensed something lost in his voice, like a child who realized his pet wouldn't live forever. She walked up to him, getting close enough to catch a strong scent of whiskey. How long had he been building up the guts to come to her? How many drinks, how many near misses?

'Things are fine, Philip,' said Nadine. She placed her hand against his chest, but kept him half an arm's length away. 'I need this trip to see my dad. Maybe I miss him more than I realized. I need to see him and figure a few things out.'

'Things?'

Nadine hesitated. Maybe Philip was safe. She wasn't her father or her mother, and Philip figured into her world a wholly different way. Then again, the drinking, the hiding of emotion behind the excuse of intoxication and the sideways entry point into whatever it was their relationship might morph into, sent her head spinning. Nadine wanted the world that she couldn't have. The one that existed before her father left, well before that night on the way back from Indy. She smiled, decided to deflect. 'My dad ran away with another man. My mom is living in denial. I'm their one and only child.' She paused. 'I've got work now,' Nadine said.

'Promise to at least have dinner with me before you head off to Oregon,' said Philip.

'Okay,' she said. She directed her gaze downward, focused on the toes of his shoes, watched as he shifted his weight. There was something about the sweet maltiness of whisky on his skin that made her want to push into him, kiss him like she had those weeks ago. But she had made up her mind already. She looked up at him, smiled an uncertain smile and walked him out of the house, still keeping a good arm's length away.

The day after meeting Philip and Erin and Red and the others at Miranda's Tavern, Nadine wakes up angry. Angry because of the conversation with her mother the night before, the same one she had all too often, about staying in Louisville, going to church, settling down. Angry because she had returned to New Albany for many of those very reasons. While church is completely off the table, she knows deep down that she had longed for the seeming predictability of her hometown and her time with Philip. The anger blooms and the realization with it that what she thought possible—what she considered the safe course in an uncertain and potentially lonely life—was nearly impossible to attain. The feeling dogs her until she wakes up determined to turn things around. It boils over towards her old friends.

She is pissed, not so much at Erin, but at Philip, for being that damned weak to hook up with someone so damned close to them all. Erin is only doing what Nadine would have done had she chosen to stay put, to lead an easier life.

'Got some tickets for the Bats tonight,' she says to Philip over the phone. 'I haven't heard you talk much about the Reds's pitching prospects. Figured it'd be nice to get some time with the expert before I head off into the sunset.' She wants to add that there are only two tickets—two tickets for them and them alone. Philip agrees and says nothing about Erin or about anyone else. He tells her he'll pick her up a good hour before the gates open because he thinks they should watch batting practice from the parking lot before the game. There's a lot to tell her about the Reds's minor league prospects.

Philip natters on about baseball and the Reds with the occasional diversion about fishing. His team has always been the Cardinals, but his job is with the Reds farm team.

Throughout the batting practice, he makes no mention of Erin, nor of the last time he and Nadine had seen each other. He insists that Nadine had missed nothing the previous evening, that the party had broken up shortly after she had left. He says that her leaving made sense. They were all sunburnt and tired and beat down from a day at the river.

They watch the game from the first base line, and the sun falls behind the trestles of the Clark Memorial Bridge far quicker than Nadine would like. The Bats dispatch the Columbus Clippers with a 7–2 outing, and while the skyline of Louisville burns in the wake of the descended sun, Nadine and Philip walk down to a bourbon bar on a street near Nadine's hotel.

They pick up where they had left off at the ballpark. Pick up at some point well before last night's well-populated gathering, pick up at sometime in the distant past. They drink eight-dollar bourbons and play catch-up with the little things they have missed over the past months. Their voices ring out more fluidly now. The lull of the middle innings has gone, replaced by the flurry that is so typical of the eighth and later innings. The world around them passes, blurred and washed out, as if they are travelling at highway speeds. Philip talks a lot about baseball, about how the Cardinals are just one key player away from the World Series, about how crap the new maple bats are, about how he wishes he could find the time to fish like he used to. It's not long before they're back to ancient history, the mythic roots of the world they had built fishing along the Ohio.

'The thing with knuckleballers is that they are so often thought of as second-rate players,' Philips says. 'Second-rate because they keep their secrets closer than most. No flashy fastball or foreseeable change-up. There's an unpredictability to what they'll do to protect those secrets. It's that unpredictability that makes them so great, though—

quietly great. It makes them untouchable because you don't know where a knuckleball is gonna land until it crosses the plate.'

'Even second-rate players have fans,' Nadine says.

'Maybe so,' he says as he leans back against the chair. 'But the crowd can turn and turn fast. They tend to turn on the ones they think are weaker, whether that weakness exists or not.'

'Like Haines?'

'ESPN said Haines is one of the most overrated players in the Hall. Assholes and their info babes.'

Nadine laughs. 'You sound like your dad,' she says.

Philip laughs.

'I still like Haines,' she adds. 'He taught me everything I can't do in fishing.'

'Seriously though,' Philip says. 'How's Oregon, and your dad?'

Nadine pauses. 'Better than here, I suppose. I'm not having to stay in a hotel out there. A lot less of ye olde Catholic guilt out there.'

'And less good old-fashioned mother-daughter fighting.'

'Again, more upside.'

'It's all about the upside out west, right? Great Hollywood dreams?' His comment stings. Nadine thinks it could have been on purpose. She doesn't want to answer him.

'We weren't....' She trails off, pauses, then rubs her thumb along the rim of the glass. 'I wasn't going anywhere here. It was time to get out, I suppose.'

'You basically told me to fuck off that night in the kitchen.'

'I was running scared,' Nadine says. 'I haven't exactly had the best role models for relationships. My dad ditched out on my mom. My mom curses him to the fires of hell at every opportunity.'

'What are you looking for?' Philip asks. Nadine is taken aback by Philip's question. It might be the only honest question that she has shared with him since the Pomegranates show in Indy.

'You mean coming back here, right?' she asks.

'Yeah, what is it with you and Louisville?'

And Nadine hears the echoes of Philip's own name under the name of the city they once shared. It is faint, though, and it makes the word ring hollow.

'I was wondering that myself. Somehow, I just can't break away from it. You know, the whole damned reason I ended up back on a plane out here was because of a baseball game on the radio.'

'Baseball?'

'The Mariners,' she says. She knows she must sound like she is snapping, as if a part of her is breaking out. 'Not the point, though. So one day I find myself standing there at the docks trying to size up the ocean and the shore for a picture, and I'm hearing this radio talk about some batter striking out, and all I can think about is Stengel and Haines.'

'My grandfather's no-hitter story?' he asks.

'Still feel like a witness to this day?' Nadine swishes back some bourbon from her tumbler. 'I'm hearing the voice and I know what he's actually talking about. But all I can remember are the times that you used to tell me the story before the game. I thought about it and realized how lonely it is out there. I didn't know the guy who owned the radio, let alone the guy who was at bat, and all of a sudden a year's worth of exile came crashing back in on me. I wanted the things I knew. I needed them.'

Philip exhales, nervously laughs. He reaches across the table and touches the warmth of his clean palm to her hand.

'You should walk me to my room,' Nadine says.

Philip agrees and they walk out of the bar. Together.

———

Philip presses Nadine against the wall of the elevator and she tastes the sweetness of shared breath in their kiss. They share and swim in frantic, growing waves of pent-up lust as the elevator ascends. They tear at each other's clothes and bodies with hungry hands. Nadine grips Philip's back, pulling him tighter into her, as if trying to force out all of the feelings they had always held so tightly inside. She tries to block out that awkward, listless last visit in her mother's kitchen, and the soft sunlight of coastal Oregon. Philip's phone rings and he pushes her off of him. She almost falls forward. He stumbles back, reaches the opposite wall as the elevator slides to a stop. He looks sad. They walk out the door into the empty hallway of the ninth floor. He has silenced the phone and is looking Nadine over.

'What?' she demands. 'For Christ's sake, what is it?'

'Look, I want this. You and me, that is. Or at least I *wanted* this.' Philip falls against the wall near a table a good number of doors away from her room. He slides down until his butt and feet are on even ground. Nadine follows him down, sitting across from him. His phone vibrates. 'I hate this thing.' He pulls the phone out of his pocket, stares at the screen.

'What?' she demands, again.

'Surprised you didn't notice,' Philip says.

Nadine bangs the back of her head against the wall. 'Fuck that,' she says. 'You and Erin, right?'

'Not like you left me for some job out in Oregon.' He says the words almost nicely, like a parent gently reminding a child about a missed alarm.

Nadine stares across at Philip. The gulf between them is immense, and Philip looks as strange as anyone she's seen in a crowd sweeping by. She was right, before. He looks so similar but is so different.

'It's all about the timing.' Philip holds the phone, flips it around. Nadine sees the name, the number. Erin Becker 518-546-0976. The bourbon has not made the screen slippery, unreadable.

Nadine feels sunk. She tries to hold it in but can't. She starts crying. Half anger, half fear. No embarrassment, no resentment. Just the burning of uncontrolled tears. Nadine buries her head between her knees. 'Shit, shit, shit,' she hears herself repeating. She feels alone in a world that has no centre.

'Nadine?' Nadine hears Philip try to comfort her from a distance. She feels his hand on her naked arm. 'I needed to see you before I left. I couldn't have that kitchen be the last time I saw you. This is how it should be.'

She feels him stand. He helps her up, and Nadine settles her weight into him.

'What's your room number?'

'Eight twenty-two.'

Nadine can't look at him. She watches as the carpet moves by under their feet. He helps her into the room, lays her on the bed and kisses her lightly on the forehead. Philip tells Nadine that things will be better, or at least she imagines that he tells her that things will be better. Nadine still can't look at him, can't do much more than bury her head in the pillow as he walks out and closes the door behind him.

———

Nadine is all cried out and heavy headed. She remembers one of the stories Philip used to tell her after they had wrapped up fishing for the day. She remembers it as she's sitting on one of the not-so-comfortable cloth chairs at Gate 22 of Louisville International Airport.

Jesse Haines was one of those throwaway ball players who, arm-chair baseball encyclopedias loved to tell anyone who would listen, had no business being part of the Hall of Fame. Haines was a knuckleballer. His pitches should have been wild, erratic, but somehow always remained on target. Yet Haines finished his career with just under a thousand strikeouts. After the no-hitter he threw in 1924—the first ever for the St. Louis Cardinals—Haines said, 'No, it's not at all about the speed. It's all about the break of the ball.' Nadine remembers how Philip tried to move his near-Kentucky drawl into something closer to Midwestern pronunciation when he recited his family story. 'You don't win twenty games on speed alone. Like you can't haul in the big ones with a hunter's eye and lightning-fast cast. It's about timing and angles.' Nadine always felt that he cut the act close—almost too close to believe that he was channelling the long-dead athlete. They would walk from the river up to the carefree main street and towards the sweat of beers at Miranda's. Close but not touching, at perfect parallel angles to the cars and walkers that passed them.

'It's all about timing, again and again,' Philip had said.

Nadine never did become a very good fisherman, even after all those years on the river. She had given up on this trip.

Jesse Haines ended his career in St. Louis, not exactly a world away from his Clayton, Ohio home. Nadine's heading back to a life as estranged from the roots of her youth as they come. She sits at the airport as another voice calls out the final boarding call for some destination that she can't make out. Nadine can't help but think about how far Philip has wandered from the life they had all shared. How far she herself has wandered. She wonders if all of this emptiness is caused by listening to an old friend talk about timing, and the importance of finishing what you started.

FROM THE BANKS OF JEFFERSONVILLE

'Hot' was the only word that Dmitri could think of as he pulled off his sweat-drenched shirt and dropped it onto the floor. The dancers around him divided and flowed and merged like swallows in a dimly lit night, their movements spurred by peels of bluegrass fiddle, the notes climbing and falling, following melodic rivulets. Strings of Edison bulb lights cast scant illumination onto the crowd below. The dancers, including Dmitri, waded through this dull light, the occasional white cotton shirt, blouse, or dress catching the eye. Dmitri would later say that the dancers moved, each of them, that is, fuelled by the desire to occupy a space as near as physically possible to another living, breathing person. A woman with short, boyish dark hair spun past Dmitri through another cluster of dancers. He watched the glinting spikes of her hair in that low devil light and could only think about the heat and that none of them could stop because, by way of the persistent shifting of bodies, the crowd had reached an equilibrium. The subtraction of just one body—the woman was bent backwards now and Dmitri fell forward resting the weight of his belly upon her—just one subtraction and the entirety of this dance would collapse. With one final, reeling note on the fiddle, the music came to an end.

'Y'all have been very attentive tonight,' proclaimed the wiry singer, clad in blue jeans and a sequined, flame-emblazoned shirt. 'Another Kentuckian cooker done gone and finished us off for the night. The band and I would like to thank you.' He raised a pitcher of water in salute to the dancers. 'The band needs a drink, you need a drink, and it's more than likely there are places all of us would like to be getting. Thank you again, Jeffersonville.'

The dancers applauded and Dmitri backed his weight off the woman before him. He looked her over. He hoped to make out her face. She seemed younger than he would have liked, but the light on the Eagles Lounge dance floor was just too damned low to make out details. He decided that the rest of her was more to his liking. Her eyes were small, her nose pretty in a way that pleased him. Dmitri pulled her back upright by the arms.

'Thanks,' she said. She straightened the back and sides of her shirt.

Dmitri's Aunt Beata had at least once told him to give an extra few moments to his final dance partner each evening, because you never know who you might bump into in the shadows of a contra dance. His Uncle Bradford, her brother, had met his wife of twenty-some-odd years by spending that few minutes chatting—he was the family case in point. In his late thirties, Dmitri had become more and more apt to follow his aunt's advice. Dmitri was, for the most part, single and melancholy, and Bradford was a happily married man.

'You seem to have lost your shirt,' the woman said and pointed rather seriously to his deeply tanned bare chest.

'It's like the band said.' He returned the boldest smile he could. 'It's hot up in here.' Dmitri looked around the dance floor where he thought he might have tossed his shirt. 'It's long gone, wherever it is.' He was both pudgy and hairy, yet carried a raw masculine charm that he liked to strut around. Losing a shirt was nothing new to him.

'You any cooler?' she asked.

'Nope, can't say that I am.' The floor around them had cleared quickly of the majority of dancers. 'But to hell with it. It's nothing more than a shirt.'

The woman grabbed him with surprising strength, pulled him alongside her and turned him about. Dmitri could smell the ballroom on her: sweet, earthy, like the steam off a country still. She was almost his height, three inches short of tall, and the smoothness of her skin as she wrapped herself around his back and arm felt young, as his first look of her had promised. A man with a large, professional-looking camera stood in front of them. Dmitri pitched out another smile and the camera flashed.

'Need your names and towns for the photo caption.' The man held out a small recorder in front of them.

'Abbie Kessler of Clarksville.' She looked back at Dmitri nervously when she said it.

'Dmitri Pentracis. Arctic Springs.'

The man with the camera and recorder turned and walked off into the shapeless bulk of stragglers. He slipped into the twilight beyond the warm hue of lights, disappeared. Dmitri felt Abbie drop her arm from around him.

'What is it,' Abbie said, 'that you're supposed to say to your last dance partner of the evening?'

'One of my aunts told us to spend a little extra time with them at the end of the night,' Dmitri answered. 'Always good to get to know people you spend some time with.'

Abbie smiled and shook her head in disbelief. Dmitri was lost as to why, but he took it for good when she smiled. 'The things you find out about people might not always be to your liking.'

'Got to figure that's why you should spend some time figuring that out,' he said.

Abbie laughed and shook her head. 'Your aunt, is she a happy woman?' she asked.

'Maybe,' he replied. 'But who am I to tell?' He took a not-so-tentative step towards her.

Abbie graced him with the half-cocked smile of a woman on the go who just found a compelling reason to stay put. She was just about to speak when her cellphone buzzed. A glance down and then back to Dmitri. She paused again as if thinking of something to say. 'Well Dmitri.' She dropped a half-bow and looked over her right shoulder. 'My ride back awaits. Maybe you'll be famous. Maybe we'll get to spend some more time together.'

Dmitri couldn't fathom why anyone would wish to be famous. He had never cared much for fame, nor thought about it much. He strutted down the sidewalk outside the Eagles Lounge, past the mostly empty parking lot to Pearl Street. The summer heat was both aggressive and stagnant. He retrieved his cellphone and fired off a message to his roommate, Fred, before stopping at a convenience store and grabbing some bottled sweet tea. He had given up on booze the week before. He felt great on the whole, but was thirstier than he ever remembered being. He thought it must be something to do with muscle memory.

Fred was getting off work at the nearby cigar bar. Dmitri asked him to meet up along the river with the hope it might be a little cooler there. He made his way to the small amphitheatre where Van Dyke Park met the waterline of the Ohio. Even there, the air was stifled by the heat. A coal barge moved upstream past the east arm of Louisville. The wake created by its slow progress left behind rippled light turned upside down. Fred sat nearer the street, at the edge of the park, on a bench overlooking an open plaza. Dmitri sat down on a bench beside his. Fred offered him a ragged t-shirt. Dmitri draped the shirt over the back of the bench.

'All these years,' said Fred, 'and we can do no better than pull coal outta the ground and burn it to keep us happy. We ain't nothing more than crude animals, man. Crude animals.'

'It's a miracle that we can move stuff like that, though.' Dmitri said. He thought only infrequently of the coal barges. They were mere accents on his daily rituals.

'Tell you what, you got that one right,' answered Fred. 'But we still need to burn that garbage just to get by, because we ain't nothing more than crude animals.'

Fred had given up the drink after being forcibly removed from the front steps of the Muhammad Ali Museum over a vending machine dispute. That was almost a year and a half ago, and ever since the moment the judge handed down his probation, Fred had given himself over to sweet tea and declarations of man's animal nature. Dmitri had followed suit after an incident at the Louisville Slugger Museum involving a Ty Cobb replica bat.

'I'll leave the positive thinking to you,' offered Dmitri.

'Just calling it like it is.' Fred stood up, walked to a nearby bush and urinated into it. 'You should know that this heat makes me damn near ornery. But suffice it to say that plenty of folk are getting pissed off by Kessler Energy. They aren't doing nothing but burning toxic crap and making sure none of us see more than a hot nickel for it. Someday someone is gonna snap.' Fred returned, close to the bench. He glanced over the river vista before him, taking it in quietly. 'Hey, how the hell was that dance of yours tonight?'

'The band was pretty good, and there were a lot of people,' answered Dmitri. 'Wish they would have spent a little extra on some lights. Darker than a cave in that place.'

'You really like that old-time music?' Fred sat beside Dmitri. A single car rattled down the street behind them, towards the bridge.

'Yeah, yeah,' he answered. 'Don't fix what isn't broken right?'

'I hear you there,' Fred replied. 'There a good story to losing the shirt this time?'

'Not really,' Dmitri said. 'Other than it was hotter than hell in there. I let it go sometime before the last song.'

'Throwing your shirt around like some hillbilly.' Fred laughed. 'You sure as shit were born to be on this riverbank.'

'What can a man be but what he is?'

'Coal-burning crude animals,' said Fred. He shook his head.

Dmitri swore he could feel the dull thrum of the barge's engines. Its steady shaking grew into a presence that made him uncomfortable. He wanted it to break as it was worse than the heat, heavier and almost aggressive in its persistence. He got lost in his discomfort. Stared at the tail end of the barge, wished for it go silent.

Fred laughed and took a big pull off the sweet tea. 'Just two past-their-prime single guys,' he said, 'sitting by the river, hiding out from the heat.'

'Ain't got no problems with that,' answered Dmitri.

He thought about telling Fred about Abbie. Dmitri had a short, unremarkable history with women. He often thought it was on account of he also had a short, unremarkable employment history. Women always preferred men with steady work, his Aunt Beata had told him. For the most part, Dmitri ran odd jobs for the slightly wealthier acquaintances he hustled up. On occasion he sold some of them insurance products. Dmitri knew that wasn't the sort of thing that lured the opposite sex his way, but it was better to know one's true self, and Dmitri knew that he was not a full-time work sort of guy.

Without the booze, he had taken to thinking more about women. Abbie was the first one in a good long time who had exchanged genuine if not pleasant words with him, let alone agreed to take a picture with him. 'Ended the night on the upside,' boasted Dmitri. 'One outstanding final dance.'

'I bet you did,' Fred ribbed him.

'No lie,' said Dmitri. 'Even got a photo to prove it. Well, not yet.'

Fred looked at him curiously. 'Yet?'

'Newspaper guy,' replied Dmitri. 'Guess is that it's that weekly arts paper from Louisville. But they got some pictures of us. Betcha they put those up tomorrow. People love watching other people having fun,' he declared.

'Well, damned if you and your girl aren't gonna be plastered all over Kentuckiana *tout suite* tomorrow morning.' Fred laughed. He had always been the type to celebrate the accomplishments of his friends with as much bravado as a Chicagoan on a bourbon tour. 'You and your shirtless warthog gut will be all over the pages, grinning away beside some pretty young thing.'

'True manhood like they never seen it.' Dmitri pulled a long haul off his sweet tea bottle. He heard talking and laughing from the nearby Big Four Pedestrian Bridge. Rich, multi-coloured lights across its large steel trusses lit the bridge enough for him to make out a sizeable group of people. He swore he saw a baseball-sized flaming object fall from the bridge towards the barge, then watched a single person run off towards the Louisville side. About a hundred feet in on his side of the bridge, he saw someone turn around and holler at the group. They walked hurriedly and seemed to signal for the group to walk back towards the Jeffersonville side. Dmitri perked up. He scanned the bridge to make sense of the warning but saw nothing. Then, the first tuft of black smoke crossed in front of the centre span. He realized the fire was coming from below.

'Oh shit,' said Fred. 'That barge is lit up.'

Dmitri, too, saw the smoke and traced it back to the barge. Neither man moved. The dull hum of the engines stopped. Dmitri could just make out a second person on the bridge, close to the spot from which he was half-certain the object had fallen. Both figures hesitated, then ran back towards Jeffersonville.

'Like it ain't hot enough?' said Fred, rattled.

They watched as the first flames emerged above the deck, coming from the side of the large mound of coal. The people atop the Big Four Bridge briskly made their way back into Jeffersonville a couple of blocks inland.

'Should we do something?' Fred asked.

'Sit here,' replied Dmitri. 'Front row seats for the show. Besides, what else we gonna do? It is fire surrounded by water. The rest is someone else's problem.'

The rest unfolded slowly, as if mired in the thickness of night. It seemed to take nearly an hour for the flames and smoke to spread to the centre of the barge. More and more black smoke obscured the bridge and the city lights behind it. A good chunk of the barge was on fire before Dmitri made out the splashes caused by the barge's crew members jumping overboard. The men were halfway to shore—the Jeffersonville shore—before the emergency vehicles descended on Riverside Drive. Dmitri and Fred hardly moved the entire time. Fred lit a cigarette and offered a drag to Dmitri, who refused it.

'Slow burner,' Fred pointed out. 'This gonna go on for a while.'

The police and firefighters were hollering at the men who had swum ashore. Other spectators began to gather around the waterfront. 'That's one of them Kessler barges.'

'Someone is gonna take a bad fall over this,' offered Dmitri.

'Looks like your late-night newsmaker dance just got booted off the front page,' joked Fred.

'Good,' Dmitri replied. 'Never been one geared for no front pages.'

'Don't think that anyone is ever geared for that sort of thing,' said Fred. 'It sort of finds you, whether you like it or not.'

By then, the barge was mostly engulfed in flames.

Morning dawned with choking, particulate-heavy light, like the worst kind of Sunday morning. Dmitri had slept till near ten a.m. Sleep had been fitful given the heat and stagnant air that even a couple of fans couldn't seem to move. He had not dreamed, not that he could recall. He found Fred sitting on a couch in the living room, three fans pointed at him, newspaper in hand. A plate of mostly-eaten toaster waffles lay on a chipped plate on the coffee table between two of the fans.

'Those square dances take a lot out of a man?' Fred joked.

'Contra,' Dmitri corrected him. He had to correct Fred almost daily on the name since taking up his dancing habit about six months prior. Although his roommate had been right about his being tired; exercise was something Dmitri had left behind after high school. The dances were something he had come to look forward to between working and going on benders. He was certain that Fred had chosen to rib him about the one thing Dmitri wouldn't get sore over. 'Barge still burning?'

'All over the news,' Fred said. 'Non-stop about the smoke and the health hazards and, you know, the usual ambulance chasing. Good news for us is the smoke is blowing towards New Albany. We get to keep our windows open.'

Dmitri retrieved a cup of lukewarm coffee and sat across from Fred in the still air behind the fans. 'Those news people rely on your crude animals for their work,' he said. 'They need fuck-ups like that boat crew to make a living off of. Made you buy a paper.' He leaned forward, retrieved an almost-full waffle and proceeded to eat it.

Fred shook his head and laughed. 'Funny you should say that,' he said. 'That girl last night,' said Fred. 'You know her name?'

'Abbie,' Dmitri replied, strangely clearheaded, as if providing the answer was the single reason he had gotten up that morning.

Fred pushed the newspaper over to Dmitri. 'Kessler?' he asked.

'Yeah,' said Dmitri. He grabbed for the newspaper, scoured the first page for a picture of her. Some part of him hoped to see their picture from the Eagles Lounge.

'Not there,' offered Fred. 'Look inside.' Three page shuffles later he found a picture of a woman he quickly recognized as her. She was standing with a well-to-do business family, clearly one of the daughters. 'Kessler as in Kessler Energy Systems.' Fred spelled it out for him. The company name was synonymous with local environmental disasters, worker deaths, and the general disregard that some of Kentuckiana's wealthiest had for anything outside of money and the large estates they could buy with it.

'What is this?' Dmitri asked.

'Kessler and Company owns that smouldering coal barge out there,' said Fred. 'People are pissed. Might have done some damage to the bridge. You can bet that this whole fire thing is a lot like the sniffer rag that the boys throw out to the dogs before they going hogging.' He sat upright, suddenly taking notice of Dmitri's serious posture. 'You were actually hooking up with a daughter of that shitbag family?'

Dmitri shook his head. 'The shitbag family,' he said. He looked over the photo of the Kesslers, paying particular attention to Abbie. She looked young. Early twenties young. Freshly minted from university young. He recognized her by the nose. She was a tad bit prettier in his memory than she was in the photo. Still though, for what passed for beauty in the blue bloods in this part of the Ohio River Valley, she wasn't half bad. 'This a problem, you think?'

'You mean getting your picture taken with an heiress the night her family pissed off all of Kentuckiana?' Fred scratched at his leg. 'Don't sound like the end of the world to me. But maybe get back with me after a minute. Things really escalate quickly in this sort of heat.'

Dmitri knew Fred was right. It was a well-known fact that the shootings in West Louisville spiked when heat like this settled in. The thick cloud of smoke rolling off the river barge added grit and an ominous haze to the heat-charged atmosphere that only seemed to make things more dangerous. For now only the possibility of cross currents could push Dmitri around, all because a picture of him and Abbie Kessler might appear in some publication, somewhere in the area. Until anything happened, like the emergence of that photo or the explosion of that coal barge in the river, all of this mattered only to Dmitri. Stories, even when they spanned a city in scope, mattered most to the characters who populated them.

He opted to carry on as if last night was a pleasant passing of sorts. A good five, maybe six fan swipes later, he made up his mind. His phone chimed in with a message request on his social media. **AbeeKessler502** had asked him to meet up with her.

About an hour later, Dmitri went down to the riverfront to meet Abbie. He hadn't told Fred out of fear that the meeting might prove more embarrassing than anything else. Instead he made an excuse about getting out of the dense heat of the apartment and finding a breeze and a sweet tea by the river. He sat on a bench upriver from the barge fire, a quiet spot not far from his place. Still, the air was thick with haze. The scent put Dmitri in mind of turn-of-the-last-century Louisville—coal burning was celebrated then as college basketball championships were now. He was certain that a sizable crowd of people would still be watching the slow-burning fire. Louisville and its Indiana suburbs were comprised of folks who watched disasters as if they were post-dinner game shows.

Abbie Kessler arrived less than fifteen minutes after Dmitri. She pulled up in a newer black German sedan. He was fairly certain that she parked illegally before getting out of the car, crossing the street and approaching him. 'I count myself as pretty lucky that there is only one Dmitri Pentracis in all of Kentuckiana on Facebook,' she said.

'My grandmother always said I was one of kind,' Dmitri replied.

'Was worried I wouldn't recognize you,' Abbie said.

'Guess it wasn't all that dark,' Dmitri joked. Abbie took a few steps closer to the bench, still keeping her distance.

'Um,' she started, 'so you haven't seen any of the—' She lost the nerve or will to finish the statement. 'You've got the social media stuff. Guess you aren't using it that much?'

'Not really,' offered Dmitri. 'Only kind of "social" I get is where I can be, you know, actually social with people. Not all typing angry on a small keyboard. Besides, everyone busy drinking and taking pictures of their food. I can get that on cable TV. But I gotta look the part. I have it. You can find me. But like I said. It ain't really me.'

'Okay,' said Abbie. 'Well, that explains you calmly sitting in the park. You know there's a barge burning in the river?'

'Yep,' he replied. 'Watched the whole thing happen last night. Actually, right after I finished dancing with you. Funny enough, I was just sitting by the river then, too.'

'Do you mind if I sit?' she asked. She motioned to the far side of bench, beside Dmitri. She sat down.

'Your people are in the coal business,' said Dmitri. 'I'm guessing your people also got something invested in that burning boat.' Abbie nodded her head. She appeared to gain in confidence. 'And you're a fine dancer,' he added. That comment elicited a smile from Abbie.

'Because of what my family is known for,' she started, 'both good and bad, at certain times I feel like I get a little too much attention. It can give a girl the worst sort of reputation.' She lingered on that last comment for a second. 'You know,' she added, 'sometimes things that are pretty normal, like going out dancing and then ending up in a local lifestyle magazine or on a website in a picture with a working-class guy. Then you've got your faces on every site.'

Dmitri took the characterization of himself as working-class as a compliment. Folks generally called him 'asshole' or 'drunk fuck' or 'lowlife'. He did work. And while it didn't by any means define the way he thought of himself, being cast as a worker brought on grand thoughts of being seen as a brawny, shirtless hero to the factory crowd. Visions of fire-cooked metals tumbling out of the furnace and then onto the assembly line, him hammering each molten bundle into perfect form with a majestic hammer. Then he thought about the picture. 'Wait,' he said. 'The picture.'

'You and me on a million or so pages,' she said. Dmitri was clearly impressed with the thought. 'We have been seen together by a lot of people on a lot of sites online. Can be a little daunting, I know. Been that way for pretty much my whole life. Being on display, that is. And I know it's not all that popular or common for people to be all out in the world. Especially for someone that doesn't take all that well to social media. So, thanks for meeting me.'

Dmitri was excited that a woman should thank him for anything. He did recognize that thank yous usually came before women asked him for things. He paused for a good moment in silence and tried to assemble the events of the previous twenty-four hours. 'So, are you saying that a lot of people are looking at the photo from last night?'

'Starting to, anyways,' offered Abbie.

His mind was racing, trying to understand exactly what all this public attention was going to end up meaning. He said nothing and bobbed his head as if in agreement—without actually agreeing to a damned thing. Surely this was heading towards a bigger change than giving up drinking or losing another job?

'Look,' she said, earnestness creeping into her voice. 'I am on my way to a press conference with my dad and brothers. It's because of the barge fire. The smoke and stuff isn't going over well, and people are already pretty pissed off at the family name because, well—'

'You make money by selling coal,' said Dmitri. 'And it's dirty.'

'My family does,' Abbie said. She was forceful in her correction. 'I've got my own life down in Asheville. Or I'm trying to, anyways. But I was thinking, though. If all you're doing is sitting here on an otherwise nothing-is-gonna-happen day, you could maybe come along.'

'To a press conference?' Dmitri asked. The request was odd but alluring. Abbie was not unattractive. Uncle Bradford would most certainly have approved of an action of this calibre. He looked her in the eyes and wanted to say he saw the lights of the dance reflecting back at him. He was ready to agree before Abbie even answered.

'It can be lonely,' she flirted, 'being the youngest daughter of a wealthy, disliked family in this part of the Commonwealth.' She leaned forward, accentuating her breasts through her simple cotton shirt.

'But we're in Indiana,' said Dmitri. He dumbly stared at Abbie's chest.

'Close enough,' snapped Abbie, losing her sweetness momentarily. 'You in?' She waited a good five, maybe seven seconds without a response from Dmitri. 'Besides, people are starting to see our picture everywhere. Let's keep them talking.'

Dmitri laughed and nodded. He knew that no one would be looking at him. The entire premise Abbie was offering—a showering of attention from an adoring public—was as unlikely as the Ohio River flowing backwards. Sitting here on the bench, hot, exhausted and short of breath from bad air would land him alone, back in the same twin bed in the same apartment he shared with Fred, the same as it had been every other night for the last few years. Not ever having been to a press conference in his life added to the allure. He agreed and he dutifully followed Abbie to her car.

The atrium of the building that housed the offices of Kessler Energy Systems was a bland leftover from the end of the last century. The interior showcased drywall, some white metal, dust-stained windows and ubiquitous potted plants from someplace almost tropical but not quite exotic. The building reminded Dmitri of a Steven Segal movie, but he couldn't place the name; they tended to all run together for him.

The drive there had been quick and ethereal, with opaque, heavy coal haze blanketing the cities. Abbie had talked about the way things could be better if only people were more than their ancestry. Dmitri had listened, piecing together the important facts carefully: that Abbie Kessler was honestly single; that contra dancing was more than just slumming it for a rich girl (she did enjoy the dances); and that she disliked alcohol intensely on account of her mother's behaviour after consuming said substance. She was also clever in the way that more honest private school graduates tended to be. Abbie mentioned she had recently graduated from a college in the Carolinas somewhere. She invited Dmitri to come and see it with her and he agreed.

A large gathering of local media milled around in the atrium. A podium had been placed near the elevators and a couple of private security guards took up a position near the elevator doors. None of the reporters took much note of his and Abbie's arrival in the tower. They were preoccupied by their phones and spinning off side conversations between each other. Dmitri noted the way others were dressed—mostly in suits and ties; he had the sudden realization that neither he nor Abbie were up to the dress code. Abbie stopped them on the periphery of the gathered media. They waited. Abbie checked her phone.

'You and your dad close?' asked Dmitri. He wanted to ask if her family was expecting them, but then he thought it might sound too accusatory.

'Biologically, yes.' Abbie scrolled through several messages on her phone. 'Looks like the family just figured out I'm home from Asheville.'

'Just figured out?' asked Dmitri.

'Yeah,' she replied matter-of-factly. 'Probably just saw our photo together in *The Rivermen*.' She laughed like a kid about to get away with something. 'I'm pretty glad I found you on my way here.'

Dmitri's head spun. None of this matched up. 'Just why are we—'
His words were cut short by the opening of the elevator door. Out
walked the family he recognized from the newspaper article that Fred
had showed him earlier. The oldest Kessler brother he recalled from a
billboard on I-65 north of Jeffersonville. They looked the part of the rich
family, every one of them. Their very appearance made Dmitri uneasy.

'To watch all the ways they are going to smoulder,' replied Abbie.
'And maybe to stoke the flames.'

Dmitri couldn't quite grasp the role Abbie wanted him to play in
this corporate melodrama. He was well known as a force of chaos in
the taverns, tourist attractions and family restaurants of some parts of
Kentuckiana, and Abbie's cagey comments hinted at an affinity with
the kind of underworld with which he was all too familiar. He had a
sick feeling that the crowd assembled at this press conference was
about to witness some turmoil. 'You didn't say nothing about fighting
with your family,' offered Dmitri.

'Didn't want to scare you off,' she replied.

Her father and mother both noticed their daughter in the crowd,
making their feelings known with determined scowls.

Walter Kessler stepped before the microphones placed on the
podium. 'Ladies and gentlemen.' He spoke with confidence that only
money could buy. 'As you are all more than aware, the S.S. Harriet
Fitzsimmons is currently smouldering in the middle of the Ohio River
due east of downtown. We at Kessler Energy are co-operating with first
responders as well as officials from both the Commonwealth of
Kentucky and the State of Indiana. The crew of the Harriet Fitzsimmons are all accounted for and are currently being debriefed by our
legal and internal investigation teams.' He continued by relaying the
technical descriptions of his company's coal barge and the safety
record of the company.

'He's lying,' Abbie whispered to Dmitri. 'About just about all of it.
It's all a show. Everyone here knows it, too.'

'I saw it happen,' offered Dmitri. Although he hadn't really seen anything that he would count as true evidence, he had witnessed that fireball dropped from the bridge. 'I mean from shore.'

'They don't even care,' Abbie said. Dmitri doubted that she had heard him. 'They are more pissed about you being here.' Dmitri looked up to meet the glares of Mrs Kessler and Abbie's older brother. 'They hate people who aren't rich or who don't have a name that can sell a newspaper or launch an ad campaign.'

'I saw it happen,' repeated Dmitri. 'I saw the burning thing from the bridge fall on it.'

Dmitri could tell he had her attention if not her gaze. She kept her eyes on her father, but the torrent of emotion within her seemed to slow. She was thinking. In the uncomfortable quiet, Dmitri recalled that he had tried to run when the Louisville Police had showed up to arrest him for destroying a crate of Derek Jeter bats with a replica Ty Cobb bat at the Louisville Slugger Museum. His attempted flight had ended poorly. Now he forced himself to repress the small nervous twitch that might have sent him running out of the atrium.

'Be careful what you admit aloud,' she replied. She paused while her father stated that the company had always maintained the highest safety standards and were looking into whether it was an act of vandalism that caused the fire. Then she smiled. 'Speaking makes things true, you know?'

Her voice had the strong snap to it that he knew wealthier people, those who considered themselves wiser, often used when speaking to working stiffs like him. And she was beautiful in that moment. Abbie was beautiful and wholesome in the way that is only possible for those raised wealthy and free from the crushing stress of life. In that she was unlike most every other woman he had met.

'I'm just a normal guy,' said Dmitri. 'Burning barges, billionaire family feuds—that sort of stuff isn't me. That's all big world, important people stuff.' He realized he was trying to find a footing in terrain that was never meant for someone like him. He had generally been the one to lead in contra dance. He had done so without thinking.

The more he considered this fact, the more he realized that he was trying to avoid panic—a panic that was partly made up of his confused, gushing attraction to Abbie. It was a fact and an emotion he could not turn from. He recognized his independent control of self was slipping away.

'That's the thing, Dmitri,' she said. 'The world is made up of small people doing small things. Then all of a sudden, one grand thing happens—like a barge burning up on the river—and all those small people start looking for something of grandeur to come out of that one big thing. But it's all exterior to us. It's just this thing that happened and that maybe made us look up from whatever it was that we were doing.'

'Like drinking a tea along the river with your roommate on a hot night,' added Dmitri. He felt himself giving in. Her story mattered; his point did not.

Abbie laughed. 'Yeah, like that. Small things end up becoming the reasons we do everything.' She paused, looked around the atrium before her. 'But those big, important things that happen, they go ahead and do what they have to do. We don't matter to them or to anyone else. The boat burns because it burns, and we do what we did that night not because of it, but because we're just two people who wanted to dance to old-time bluegrass.'

'Small people doing small things,' repeated Dmitri. 'If you're into those things.'

'I am,' Abbie said. 'Very much so.' She reached down and grabbed hold of his hand. Her palm was warm, and while she was a good number of years his junior, he recognized that the strength in it far surpassed his own. 'You were with me last night,' she said. 'We saw the barge catch fire.' The way she looked at him, all wide-eyed and earthy and damned beautiful, was a late July sunrise over the Ohio.

It was the small things, yes. And yes, telling that story, the one about them watching from shore when that barge caught fire, would be such a small thing. Telling it would make it true.

Dmitri nodded. He smiled back. Abbie nestled her head against his shoulder. She didn't let go of his hand. She watched her family's press conference, then led Dmitri out of the building before the flurry of reporter questions descended. Dmitri knew the family had seen him, knew they were angry at the presence of their daughter's working-class boyfriend.

Abbie and Dmitri drove back across the river to Jeffersonville through the slow-clearing smoke of the smouldering barge.

'What am I to you?' asked Dmitri.

'The best alibi a woman can ask for,' she answered.

WON'T BE IN HARD LUCK NO MORE

The rain had been coming in heavy the past few days. The unending storm hadn't brought the steady torrential downpour stuff of Noah and his big ole boat, nor was it the kind you would associate with God tossing his wrath against the keel of said boat. Nope, it was more like the kind that came from God leaving the showerhead open just enough so that the earth became a drizzled-out swamp, an artifact of the divine at its most forgetful. You could say that places like Wheelerville, Indiana were little more than afterthoughts to a God that preferred to fill its time with thoughts of prettier and more famous locales. Another full day of toothache-grey skies above this Southern Indiana town continued with a steady rain that had begun to back up in large pools from the storm drains to the curbs. The rain had turned the grass, bushes and trees into a hue of green that taunted the threatening sky.

On the porch of an inherited house, Mason and Owen attempted to escape the humidity and heat that had built up inside over the last few days. Mason imagined a slight westerly breeze moved over their porch in the afternoons. Owen thought Mason felt what he wanted rather than what was really there, but joined him on the porch because, despite the stagnant nature of the Wheelerville air, it did manage to feel a little less oppressive out there. Both men were at the start of a two-week layoff from work as cellphone tower servicemen. They had spent the first day of that layoff quietly suffering through the aftermath of a hard night at the only tavern in town. Then they became quiet, like little boys who had run out of the ways and means to challenge the world they lived in.

And the rain kept coming. It felt like a Big Joe Williams tune about sharecroppers and failing dams and the way that even the wrong kinds of love can make a man happy enough. The steady music of water returning to earth led Mason into daydreams like the ones he'd had as a teenager listening to Delta blues records his grandfather had brought up from the South.

Edison Prestwood had followed the promise of high-paying work on the Wheelerville Dam and had settled in nearby Linton. If he couldn't keep his Bolivar, Mississippi home, he had at least carried the sounds of it with him. Mason had spent great portions of his youth with his grandfather. He listened to stories about people and places that were familiar in the kind of ways that mark ancestry over experience. Their stories, their songs, their histories pooled into a lake of prehistory, a wash of everything that had come before, both good and evil, that provided the thread to bind him to family he could never know. And those dirty blues records spun on, overlaying that threadwork and those good times and bad times, anchoring him to a world well marked by trial, disaster and migration.

It was about the sixteenth verse of that tune when *she* showed up, again. Ericka Knightlinger, the town bicycle, ran up the sidewalk from the direction of Main Street with the tot-tot-splash of white sneakers on water-logged sidewalks. Although pretty by most standards, she was petite, almost downright scrawny, with the air of a scorned castoff. Mason had joined her passenger list the previous night. A night that had left him fuzzy headed and sitting dazed on his front porch in the relentless rainstorm. Even once she had crested the stairs of the porch, panting about the imperative thing that they must be doing instead of waiting out the rain, her appearance felt out of place, like the slow-rolling approach of a landslide. Mason stared at her without comprehending her words; he heard nothing beyond her tone. She was drenched. And definitely pretty enough—large brown eyes underscoring the importance of what she had to say. The old plaid work shirt stuck close to her waif-thin frame and the naked flesh of her legs and arms shone clean. Her presence made Mason feel all the dirtier for not having showered that morning.

'Say what?' asked Owen.

Ericka let out a long, exasperated puff. 'A big tree on Lynnehurst fell right over onto the cell tower,' she said. 'It's totally busted up—too much rain. It fell over, roots and all.' She was out of breath as she spoke.

'What the hell I care?' replied Owen. He sounded more ornery than should any man in his early thirties. 'We got the day off and ain't nobody paying me to care about no damned tower.' He stood up from the plastic chair. 'You leaving a lake on my porch.' He went inside the house, leaving a disappointed-looking Ericka. A small puddle of water had formed around her feet.

'Owen sure isn't friendly today,' she said.

'Is he ever?' replied Mason. Not that she would know. He had become used to explaining Owen's short temper to friends and acquaintances for the better part of two decades. Friendly was not a word he used often, if at all, when speaking of Owen, whose recently displayed bluster was far from unusual. 'But why you come running up here all crazy as a possum in daylight?'

'Like I said.' Ericka was still attempting to catch her breath. 'The tree on Lynnehurst. You know the big ol' beech tree that eats up half of the corner? That one fell over and crumpled the cellphone tower.' She looked at him with wide, childlike eyes, and all Mason could think about was the fact that everyone's hair looked dirty, like mud across car doors, when it got wet. He had the feeling that Ericka was only telling half-truths.

The door to the house opened and a towel flung out from behind it, hitting Ericka where she stood. 'Dry up,' Owen hollered from inside the house. 'I got all the water I can take falling from the sky.' He turned around and walked back into the house. He had likely figured Ericka had come to talk to Mason alone.

Mason and Ericka had had a go around in a janitor's closet the night prior, during the celebration of Owen and Mason's layoff, maybe sometime around the seventh inning of the Reds game on the tavern's single TV. Normally that kind of thing didn't really faze Elvis Mackall, the owner and sole full-time bartender of Dutchey's Tavern. But last night Elvis had made them pay their tab early, like he knew they'd be getting into trouble that night.

Problem was that Ericka was, and still is, no more than twenty-years of age. Elvis had let her hang out in the bar on account of the rain and on the condition that she behaved herself. Mason had given more thought to Elvis's reaction than he had to the hazy drunk sex he'd had with Ericka. He had thought little of her, actually, brushing off their encounter as nothing more than his turn in line. She had told him that he was the oldest man she had been with by at least a decade. He still wasn't sure if she'd meant it as a compliment or a complaint.

Ericka took the towel and wrapped it around her head and tucked her hair up in it. 'You were saying last night that you two fixed cell towers.' She wrung out the front of her shirt before quickly running the towel over her torso. 'Figured you would be the ones to tell. We got no cellphone service in town now.' She moved gingerly and sat beside Mason on the porch swing. He could smell her hair; it was a sort of vanilla—the kind of scent that young women with a little bit of extra money bought through mail order. Mason loved the scent. It made Ericka seem more than just pretty. He was surprised to find it pleasant sitting beside her, alone, in the daylight.

He realized that he had fallen awkwardly silent.

'The hell any of us cares about cellphones,' said Owen. He emerged from the house with three cans of Falls City and distributed them accordingly. Mason received his passively, as one would a freshly lit smoke. Ericka was slow to grab hers. Owen sat down heavily in the plastic chair across from them.

Ericka put a lot of effort into pulling the tab back on her beer. She took a swig as if it were communion wine—a taste of salvation amid this meteorological act of God. 'They got a state trooper right in front of the heap of metal,' she continued. 'He's looking real busy with flares all over the place and lights flashing.'

'So, you ran over here in the middle of a rainstorm to tell us about a tree that fell over?' Mason asked, all calm-like. He rocked the porch swing as he spoke and found that he wasn't at all annoyed with her presence. He was just unsure about the earnestness of her declared intentions. He had not maintained much trust for women since Meredith, his one-time fiancée, had run off with that lawyer from Terre Haute.

Ericka sat confidently on the porch swing beside him, thumbing the rim of the beer can. She was a story. One that elicited a certain concern in him. That story might say something about his interest in a much younger woman, about the way both he and she knew most of the tri-county area in a very carnal way. That story, all of it, ran afoul of the reinforced sense of normality that existed in TV sitcoms and church pews. As far as Mason could tell, Ericka wasn't the type to be too plugged into the town rumour mill, nor was she one to genuinely care about the gossip if she were.

'Just figured you would give a damn,' she said. 'Ain't it true a real man takes pride in his work?' Her gaze remained fixed on Mason as she spoke. She looked different than he remembered from last night at Dutchey's. Maybe everyone looked younger after running around in a rainstorm, but Mason thought that Ericka looked uncomfortably young. She was something of a pale wood nymph, tiny and determined, that had appeared on his and Owen's porch in the dullest moments of their current layoff. Her presence unnerved him a little more than he imagined it should. The way her drenched shirt clung to the curves of her small breasts and slight shoulders ... he felt like he wanted the previous night to happen all over again.

'There are a lot more important things in life to be doing than thinking about work,' answered Mason.

'It doesn't much look like you're doing anything important today,' she said.

'We're drinking beer,' said Owen. 'Something I consider to be a degree or so more important than running out into the rain.'

Ericka had the look of a kid whose plans just went suddenly and inconceivably sideways. She flicked the tab of her beer can with her thumb. It sounded like bullfrogs at sunset. She sat back and folded her legs under herself, formulating some new plan. Mason lost any focus he might have concocted to speak to her. He stared and hoped to wait out whatever it was she was plotting.

'Now, Ericka Knightlinger,' said Owen, 'just what is it you're after coming here? I'd bet a Friday night at Dutchey's it's all about the fine lump of a man you have sitting beside you.' The heat or the hangover had gotten to Owen. It was clear from his tone that any answer Ericka gave was intended to provide Owen with a necessary diversion from the fierce misery of a hangover in a subtropical Southern Indiana rainstorm.

Ericka turned briefly sheepish, but did not redden from embarrassment.

Mason and Owen had been at Dutchey's Tavern in the town square when the idea of dinner and happy hour had turned into a full Reds game on TV and nearly fifteen dollars in the jukebox. In the space of three and a half hours, Mason and Owen had built a day's pay worth of a bar tab. Mason, in his enthusiasm for a three-run Scott Rolen opposite field home run, had cozied up to the only woman in their age-range at Dutchey's.

In a town the size of Wheelerville, you had to say that most everyone knew of everyone else. Such was the case with Ericka Knightlinger. It had been the better part of a decade since Mason had gotten blackout drunk, and that particular night he had gotten most of the way there. It was more selective-memory drunk—he remembered the Reds winning and the softness of Ericka's naked flesh, but not the loud and tiring sex they had had in the janitor's closet of the bar. There was something in the way she looked at him, both now and the previous night, that said she didn't forget details. In those forgotten details there was something important that Mason knew he should have remembered.

'You both graduated from Linton, right?' Ericka asked. Linton was the bigger, richer school one township over, the one that generally beat up on Wheelerville's smaller, much more poorly funded sports teams.

'Sure did,' said Owen. He leaned forward like he was getting ready for some type of proclamation.

'I am a Wheelerville girl through and through,' she proclaimed. 'I was even a cheerleader.' She sat up proud as she said it and looked over at Mason. 'We'd do our thing while your boys just kept running the ball into our end zone.' She laughed. 'Our boys weren't none too good.'

'Don't doubt they still aren't,' said Owen.

'Wheelerville is you boys' town too, now,' she reminded them.

'Maybe. We live here now,' said Owen. 'But you'd be hard-pressed to get Mason to follow no other football team. He was a letterman.' He pointed at Mason for added emphasis. 'Right there is Southern Indiana's strongest hitting free-safety in the last forty-five years.'

Ericka looked Mason over with hungry eyes.

Last night had been all small talk about the baseball game and the trivial things that came up during the commercials. Mason was comfortable with that. But he hated that today's conversation had directed attention to his past.

His entire football career had ended badly. It was a mix of everything that an after-school special showed you not to do, minus the drugs and addictions. Looking back, it was a time marked by a series of bad decisions, from choosing a high school sweetheart over a University of Evansville scholarship to a half-hearted apprenticeship in cabinet making. Those decisions landed Mason in this exact moment, on a porch in Wheelerville, with a lover who was closer to being a girl than a woman and a rainstorm that seemed like it would never end. Instead he focused on the material of Ericka's shirt as it clung, drenched, to the curve of her breasts. She caught him staring, gave a small, tight smile, and then shifted her hands to her lap, still clutching the beer can. Mason nodded.

'I might have seen you play a couple of times,' she said. 'But I was just a kid back then. Everyone seemed like a superhero.'

The thought of Ericka as a kid at one of his high school games unnerved him. Made him feel old and dirty—like some of the slightly older grads he and his teammates had joked about back in the day. He knew that Ericka had come to their porch in the middle of the great deluge from the forgetful Lord not because a tree had hit a cell tower, and not to rehash some Southern Indiana high school football history.

Mason had heard about how Wheelerville girls were coy and sneaky, and how you were always better off knowing that they looked out only for themselves, because that is what small-town girls with no future past high school cheerleading had to do. He stood up from the porch swing in a moment of discomfort. The rain began hammering down harder. He looked back at Ericka. She was pretty. Damn it.

'I got some drier stuff you can put on,' he said to Ericka. 'Sure it's hot out, but sitting there in soaking-wet clothes isn't going to do you any favours.'

Ericka motioned to Mason with a playful grin and eyes the colour of freshly turned soil. 'Whatcha gonna look at, then?'

Owen laughed loud and hard.

'Same thing as before,' replied Mason, 'just in one of my shirts.' He recognized the game. No need to make timid about it.

Ericka beamed a wide, very white smile and picked at her beer can tab.

'So that's it,' said Owen. 'You're here to get you some seconds.'

'Fuck you, Owen,' said Ericka. She stood up and followed Mason inside. 'I knew you was looking too. But washed-up musicians just ain't my type.'

Ericka followed Mason into the small Depression-era bungalow. It was dark, like the cavernous shadows of black-and-white WPA photos of rural poverty from the 1930s. The wood-panelled walls caught what little light entered the room. Neither Mason nor Owen considered art or decoration high priorities. The room was spare in the kind of way hotel rooms generally are. This, despite the fact they owned the home and had for the better part of four years. They treated it like a flop house—a waypoint between work, travel, hotels and bars.

'This place sure looks small on the inside,' Ericka declared as she passed through the small living room into Mason's bedroom. She rubbed down the ends of her hair with the towel. The sound of rain falling on saturated earth trickled in from an open window at the back of the room. The paltry amount of breeze it let pass left the air inside still and heavy, as if the room had been lived in for too long.

'Well,' Mason replied, 'it's a roof over our heads.' He had promised her a change of clothes, and he was just now trying to figure out how to fulfill that promise. He went through some dresser drawers looking for old t-shirts and some boxers that were both not embarrassing and easy to part with.

'I didn't mean nothing by it,' Ericka said. 'Looks a lot like one of my uncle's places down in Jeffersonville.'

'Neither one of us is too good with the housekeeping stuff,' said Mason. There were used t-shirts and shorts in piles and scattered on the floor. A few used cups and bowls lay alongside magazines and dime store–sized books. He pulled a barely worn Purple Aces shirt from the dresser. It was as old as the offer he had received from Evansville. He remembered the afternoon he had bought the shirt: bright, sunny, a few days after he had first heard from the university and about a month before Meredith told him she wasn't going. He had held on to it all these years, never really wearing it. The shirt held all the memories of a life unravelled. He handed the grey-and-purple t-shirt to Ericka as if it were a state championship trophy.

Ericka took it and unfurled it unceremoniously in front of her before dropping it on the mattress. The mattress lay on the floor, topped with balled-up sheets and pillows. 'Well it sure ain't no trailer.'

She sounded resigned as she spoke, somewhat like overburdened royalty surveying her kingdom. She lifted her soaked shirt over her head and discarded it onto the floor. Mason's gaze lingered for a moment on her exposed stomach. He turned and sifted through the top drawer to find shorts or a pair of boxers.

'Did you think about ever calling me?' Ericka asked. The question was more probing than accusatory in its tone. He turned to find her pulling her hair back into a bun. She was wearing the t-shirt, and the bottom hem rested just above her middle thigh. The Purple Aces letters bent low over her chest like a frown. Mason couldn't get over how diminutive she appeared. He felt uncomfortable and somewhat guilty for the things they had done—and might have done—at Dutchey's. He could not fathom an appropriate response to her statement. He handed her a pair of blue plaid boxers.

'No point pretending,' Ericka said. 'I'm pretty used to the one-night thing.' She handed over the balled-up mass of her wet clothes. Her voice was matter-of-fact, her outstretched hand demanding.

'Ain't no one pretending,' Mason replied. 'You really have to give a man a couple of days to let stuff sink in.' And then he knew he was lying. He had never had any intention of doing much in the way of thinking about Ericka. He had felt embarrassed and little sick from the hangover. But a whole lot of that embarrassment stemmed from what Elvis might think of Mason and what he did in Dutchey's bar. Elvis was an old stalwart of Wheelerville's social network. A lot of the important news about the residents of the town and surrounding counties passed through him. Mason figured that he and Ericka could just move on and stumble through the rest of their lives, their encounter little more than a short, seedy footnote in the book of Wheelerville lore.

'You got a clothes dryer in here?' Ericka asked. She still held her balled-up clothes in one outstretched arm. Mason traded them for a pair of boxers. Ericka finished dressing and followed him through the house to the mudroom that housed their laundry machines. 'I know about your ex-fiancée,' she said, 'and it doesn't bother me.'

'Who the hell doesn't?' Mason snapped. He was tempted to ask how she knew; then he realized that Elvis had likely told her when he and Owen weren't at the tavern.

'Not all us women are that shitty,' she said. She had such sweet brown eyes, the colour of the Wabash on the right hot July day. Mason was sure she wielded those eyes like a weapon.

'Is that why you're here?' Mason asked. He refused to address the comment about his ex-fiancée. 'Because you thought I wasn't going to call you back?'

'Maybe,' Ericka said. She paused to look over the front of the t-shirt again. 'But there is still a downed cellphone tower and there ain't a way to get a hold of no one. But if you want to believe I'm here because I'm nothing more than a clingy one-night stand, that's up to you.' She hovered next to Mason as if to elicit his faith with proximity and sheer force of will.

'So, this is coming down to what I believe?' Mason asked.

Ericka followed him back into the kitchen. The clouds outside the windows had begun to grow darker.

'Would you have called?' she said.

'What do you think?' Mason replied.

'I ran to your house in a rainstorm,' Ericka replied. There was a cutting sincerity in her voice; it put Mason in mind of a coach trying to explain the nickel defense to a cheerleader. 'We all do things that we don't understand sometimes. We just like to hope there is a good reason why.'

Mason surveyed her, from her towel-wrapped head to the smooth flesh of her legs. Her eyes had a playful if not hopeful look. His shirt was at least two sizes too big on her, but the dirty grey and the purple letters matched in some unlikely way. The moment seemed right. She should have been in his t-shirt long ago.

'What is it?' she said.

He didn't immediately know how to answer her. Mason could hear the rain hitting the roof and the sound of the dryer as it tumbled away in the room behind them. What was the matter with him? Why did this particular woman get to him? There had been others since Meredith had run off. Other one-night stands in Greencastle, Vincennes and Rockville—and those had left no effect on him. On the rare occasion the other party had called or come looking for him, he had not wanted to see them again. But Ericka was different somehow, and becoming more and more interesting to him by the minute. 'Why did you run here?' he asked.

Ericka grasped the fabric of his shirt in her clenched fist and pulled him closer. She was quite a bit shorter than Mason. Her forehead barely met his chin, so she had to tilt her head back as she approached. Ericka glared defiantly. This was the closest he remembered being to her. 'You best not think it's all about that cell tower,' she said in a half-threatening, half-playful voice.

Owen hollered from the front porch. His muffled words were followed swiftly by the sound of two vehicles moving rapidly through the waterlogged street. Mason glanced back towards the living room. In between more hollered words, Mason could feel Ericka's breath against his neck. When he faced her, she was pouting at him, taking great offence at his distraction.

Owen came through the front, announcing his arrival with a loud slam. 'You see those boys flying down the street?'

Before Mason could answer, the tornado sirens growled to life outside. They wailed big and green and full of nerve-rattling summer fervour, a hellish cacophony unleashed into the superheated air over this small Indiana town, as if to wash its wretched little homes and streets away with the wrath of an awakened, alert and wrathful God.

It was then that Ericka kissed him. The kiss was deep and encompassing and tasted of warm cotton candy. In it he found an excited familiarity, like a pleasant childhood memory, that made him grab at her waist. She felt boney and fragile, but strong and certain in the way she controlled her movements. She let out a small giggle and released him. Owen was in the doorway of the kitchen near the stove, and he looked at them both impatiently. The tornado sirens were wailing.

'Figured you two were sober,' joked Owen. 'Quite a few big rollers from the state troopers just went blazing towards downtown.'

The tornado sirens sounded so frequently this time of year that Mason had learned to tune them out, for the most part. The piercing tone elicited an alertness in some animal nerve reflex that Mason would have preferred not to call fear. Maybe it was the little cloud of the unfathomable that every kid growing up at the end of the Cold War carried into adulthood. Maybe it was the way every newscaster and parent portended that the end would come by twister.

'Sirens could be anything,' Mason said. 'And it doesn't feel like tornado weather. It's too lazy.' He looked back at Ericka. 'So, you didn't come here 'cause the cellphone tower was down?' he asked.

'No, you idiot,' she said. 'I came here because I wanted to see you. Cellphones weren't working and I got sick of waiting around in an empty trailer.'

'The fuck you two?' asked Owen, who shook his head. He turned back into the living room and switched on the radio. They had no TV in the house. The last one had been a Goodwill shop special and had blown out months back. Outside, the heavy rain continued unabated, its consistency only underlined as the sirens blared on.

Mason squirmed to free himself from Ericka's grasp. A feeling of guilt grew inside him, because of her youth more than anything else. He felt like he was toying with a girl altogether too innocent for the likes of him. Ericka had a reputation among the slightly younger generation of men in Wheelerville, but Mason was beginning to think maybe he should behave a little better than those men. He felt as though he owed Ericka something. The feeling surprised him—he hadn't considered any woman since Meredith to be deserving of it.

'Hang in here,' Mason said. 'Let's make sure we aren't in too much official trouble before we get further in.'

He joined Owen in the front room. On the radio, a deadpan DJ was announcing flash flood warnings and evacuation orders for surrounding counties. Mason paid close attention when Wheelerville came up in the list. Before Mason could speak or even put together a single coherent thought about the order, Owen said, 'Get your girlfriend. Let's see just what those troopers' cars are up to.'

They struck out from the house with an umbrella that Mason's older sister had given him for Christmas a few years back. In all honesty, Mason couldn't recall even opening it up since that Christmas Day. The umbrella was the black of wet asphalt with a deep-coloured wood handle—the kind of umbrella one would expect to see in an Agatha Christie mystery. Ericka had commented on the umbrella's stark opulence and had swiped it when they had walked out onto the porch. She carried it with her arm held up high, as if to offer enough space to accommodate the much taller men around her. Despite her all-too-baggy men's clothes, plaid boxers and all, she remained fixed to the dead centre of the umbrella's rain shadow, perhaps fearing a reprimand from Owen, perhaps already proving her point about alerting them to the dangers of this rainstorm. Owen had surged ahead a couple of paces in what was now a shiny and very wet green raincoat. Mason was close by Ericka, partially in the cover provided by the umbrella.

The trio crossed Second Street and rounded the next block to Sycamore Street, making their way to the town square. They walked because Ericka insisted that both Mason and Owen were too drunk to drive. Then they crossed Sycamore Street right near Windsor Place, Wheelerville's largest apartment building. Situated beside the old courthouse, the four-story brick-and-glass structure was a relic of the coal boom in the 1950s. So often it looked empty, but now, in the gloom of the never-ending rain, Mason could make out the lights in most of the apartment windows.

Wheelerville had entered an unending blue hour. It felt as if the whole town was just about to get up from a heavy sleep after a night that had almost done it in. But the tornado sirens had been sounding for well over fifteen minutes, and it appeared at this point lost on the remaining residents of Windsor Place. They'd heard more tornado sirens in their lives than ice-cream truck bells, yet Drumsticks and Creamsicles were much more vivid in their memories than funnel clouds and green skies.

'No one seems none too worried about these sirens,' said Ericka.

'You figure they should be?' asked Mason.

'Things just seem different,' Ericka said to Mason. 'Like this isn't just any old day.'

She finished her sentence as the group turned to face the cause of the sirens' wail. A sinkhole had eaten up a large chunk of the wide road, sidewalk to sidewalk. The two-storey former dollar store building was pitched towards the street. A couple of streetlights and telephone poles teetered at near forty-five-degree angles at the edges of the hole.

Ericka made it to the sinkhole first. She was a good five, almost six, feet in front of Mason and Owen. She stopped in a puddle on the sidewalk and stood like a princess before her kingdom, her arms out from her sides as if to push it all back together. Across the gap, the two state trooper patrol cars had their lights rolling. Blue and red cycled sharply through the falling mist of rain. The patrol cars' position, haphazard and at angles, told Mason that they had arrived on land that no longer existed; the sinkhole must have recently ripped open.

'Holy fuck,' proclaimed Owen. He was directly beside Mason and a little more out of breath. 'I always called this place a hole, but this looks like a Bruce Willis movie set.' The streets were empty, as was usual in downtown Wheelerville. The only signs of life were the three of them and the two empty patrol cars.

Mason grabbed a hold of Ericka's wrist. It was hot to the touch. He pulled her back from the leading edge of the sinkhole. She fought for a moment, but eased back towards him. 'We're not going diving,' he said.

He looked over the edge. The hole went down a good fifteen feet or so. A strong current of water cut through the centre of it, flowing rapidly downgrade and pulling at the loose soil and collapsed asphalt portions of the street. He was in awe of the rushing water, the sound of it. Raw it ran, dark and fast.

'Where do you suppose all that water is coming from?' asked Ericka. 'It ain't rained that hard.'

Mason thought for a good moment. She was right. It had rained this much or more several times in his memory, and never had a sinkhole ripped open anywhere in the county. Although the rain *had* been more frequent than he would have liked ever since spring. He glanced across the sinkhole and up the road, following the way that Wheelerville climbed uphill, its low buildings pushed up towards the hills beyond. He suddenly recalled the dam, just on the outskirts of town. He and Owen had been up there a couple of days back and noticed the water was high, touching the roots of some big old trees. 'That tree you came hollering about, where was that at?' Mason asked.

'Up over at McHale Street,' she said. 'You know, uptown.' Dutchey's was uptown, in a residential part of Wheelerville defined not by wealth or prestige but by its physical elevation; it was simply higher than the rest of the town. Ericka pointed at the familiar area across the sinkhole, towards a section of climbing road. Mason squinted through the depths of the falling rain and could make out a bunch of toppled trees a couple of blocks back. The realization hit him hard.

'It's the fucking dam,' Mason said. 'It's old as anything. That piece of crap is going to give.'

Both Ericka and Owen appeared doubtful. The notion that something as everlasting as the town dam could fail was nothing that could find a footing in the unending present of Wheelerville.

'Owen, we saw the water level up there almost a week ago. All this rain—you gotta know it's not holding. I mean, look at this. This isn't from a simple rainstorm.' He gestured to the sinkhole before them.

'Where you suppose the troopers are?' asked Owen. 'You figure they would be standing around to tell us to get lost.' Owen walked to the edge of the sinkhole. 'You know, if that dam failing thing is true—'

'It is pretty quiet,' offered Ericka.

Mason scanned the horizon. As if on cue, a few cars drove towards the main street before stopping abruptly, their occupants noticing the sinkhole from above. He could make out shouting between the cars but not specific words. They turned and then sped off towards the hills above the town with clear urgency.

'Y'all see that?' asked Ericka.

'I don't like that one bit,' said Owen.

'My place is over there,' said Ericka. 'My dad might be there.'

'He has ears, doesn't he?' said Owen. 'He can hear the sirens as good as us.'

'He ain't exactly right in town,' Ericka answered.

'Even if he was,' Mason replied, 'I doubt he's thinking the same thing we thought of them.' He surprised himself by thinking of Ericka first, about how she had to be worried about her father and her place.

'Well, shit,' Owen said, then laughed a little. 'You want to go running in?' He kicked some loose asphalt towards the sinkhole at his feet. 'I'm game.'

Across the way, a pair of state troopers emerged from a two-storey building, accompanied by two families with their pets. Mason recognized a few from the gas station and from Doris's Grill. They were among the less well-heeled of Wheelerville society, the kind of people who made up the majority of the town's residents. The group paused, gaped down at the sinkhole then back across the gap at Mason, Owen and Ericka. The troopers ushered the families to their patrol cars.

'That looks serious,' said Owen.

A bone-jarring cracking emanated from the nearby dollar store. The noise built slowly at first. Then what sounded like a cascade of snapping boards gave way to the loud, ground-shaking collapse of the structure into the great maw of the sinkhole. Chunks of earth and roadway followed it in.

Owen took a few quick steps back from the lip of the sinkhole. Ericka nuzzled backwards into Mason, who wrapped an arm around her tightly. No one spoke. The water and current at the bottom of the hole had grown in depth and ferocity, sweeping away the former dollar store as if it was never meant to have existed.

'It's time to move!' The state trooper's voice boomed from the patrol car's loudspeaker. 'Evacuate the town. It is not safe here.' The trooper punched the siren three times to add emphasis. Both cars drove off in the direction of the hills.

'You heard the trooper,' said Mason. 'We best get moving. Ericka, show us your dad's place.'

———————————

The grass leading up to the front of the double-wide was saturated. Though the heavy rainfall had stopped, a steady mist continued to float down from the dark grey sky above. Mason, Owen and Ericka were about a half-mile from the highway that cut north of uptown and into the hills nearest the lip of the dam. Owen had driven them around the sinkhole at the centre of the town via empty side streets. The car had floundered in a heavy mud patch and, rather than digging or pushing it out, they opted to walk. They had agreed that the trailer was likely high enough in the hills so as not to be swallowed whole by a flood.

Ericka led them to the front door of the trailer. She had begun to look like the water-logged waif that she was when she had first showed up at Mason's place. The umbrella had been lost on the way to collect the car. Owen kept pace in the middle, trying to make the most of what he would have called an adventure in their high school days. Mason was last in line.

Outside the clearing inhabited by the trailer, the world seemed improbably distant. Rainwater sang a backwoods hymn—too quietly—as it fell off saturated leaves and branches and onto the thick grass and mallow beneath them. None of them could hear the sirens from the town below.

Ericka stumbled as she turned to face Mason. 'Dad's always got his records up so loud he probably didn't hear the siren,' she said. There was an excitement in her voice akin to a kid about to show off a new puppy. 'I know this wasn't his weekend with my Uncle Fred.' Ericka caught her footing, gave up and faced forward. 'Been too rainy for any good reason to head to Palmyra.'

Owen slowed down to let Mason catch up. 'Fuck a gal in a janitor's closet one night and, next thing you know, she's taking you home to meet Dad,' Owen whispered to him just softly enough for the hiss of the rain to drown out the words.

Mason glared and kept moving. 'Trailer in the woods part should worry me,' he said. He was beginning to suspect that the entire chain of events that had led to the trailer on the outskirts of town was all part of a sinister plan devised by a devil woman to entrap him. While he would have preferred to retreat to the car in its mud puddle parking spot, he found himself playing along with her game, partially because he found the gal to be worthy of an eyeing up, but also partially because the single man's life full of work and drink was anything but exciting. Mason followed Ericka towards her trailer home and her obstinate father because of his growing certainty that there was much, much more to life, and he was damned well going to find it.

Ericka regained a confident stride as she reached the first rotting wood step that led to the front door of the trailer. At least, Mason assumed it was the front door because he didn't see any others. He had never lived in a trailer, and he had spent relatively little time with those who did. Wheelerville and the hills around it had more of them and their hard-luck inhabitants than his part of the county. The general shape of the mobile home had a flat, leftover-factory-floor look, and as he got closer, Mason came to the realization that neither time nor the woods around them had treated the trailer well. The exterior looked like the gravel shoulder of the interstate near Indianapolis.

'Dad!' Ericka hollered and swung the door open with a metal pop. 'The storm's gone and wrecked the dam up—' She stopped mid-sentence, in the middle of the tiny kitchen of the trailer. Mason and Owen followed her through the open door. Inside the sound of a nearby box fan replaced the hollow patter of raindrops. The trailer was stale and hot like the inside of a discarded tin can. 'Well hell,' she said. 'He's already cleared out? Now ain't that love?'

The trailer smelled of incense, the kind the head shop in Vincennes would burn. A couple of rock posters— Nazareth, King Crimson and a truck stop crushed-velvet Led Zeppelin poster—occupied the walls of the living room otherwise given over to family portraits or hand-me-down artwork. The furniture, what little there was, was desperately out-of-date, the past-its-prime type of stuff that Mason's family would have left beside the road rather than pawn off on less fortunate relations.

For the first time, Mason saw Ericka in the context of the world from which she had come: a dingy metal box on the edge of town, dark, silent, and full of the discarded things that the rest of society, those back inside the town itself, would have rejected out of self-respect.

Ericka stood in the middle of her dad's kitchen, one hand half-rolled into a fist and the other rubbing slowly against her downwardly extended arm. She looked dejected, almost defeated, in the kind of way that Mason had always imagined poor children would look on gift-free Christmas mornings.

'Any pop?' asked Owen. He walked over to the fridge and opened it as if he owned it and all its contents. The fridge interior was mainly yellowed light and empty shelves. 'Would you look at that? He took the beer.'

'Dad doesn't drink,' Ericka replied coldly.

Owen said nothing in response. He closed the fridge door, walked across to the two-seat dining room table and sat down in one the chairs. The thick plastic of the chair groaned under his weight.

'You suppose he just stepped out?' asked Mason.

'He said he was thinking about leaving,' said Ericka. 'But he always said that kind of thing. I told him about meeting you in town. He sounded more eager about clearing out.' She looked up at Mason in her best tough kid kind of way and shrugged a little. 'It was because of you, but not you by name. He accused me of whoring around like my mother and her sisters.'

The old man had likely been somewhat correct. Not that Mason knew Ericka's mother—to the best of his knowledge, fewer people talked of her than of her daughter. Her aunts were equally a mystery. But he had fucked Ericka in the closet of a run-down hick bar. Reality, as always, felt harder than it should. Everything was tinged with the type of moral shadows that crept into the lives of men more successful than him. Owen looked at Mason and shook his head. Ericka caught him.

'Hate to break this up,' said Owen, 'but we've got this whole dam-failing thing going on as we speak. I do hope your dad is just fine. But I'm thinking we should be getting out from in front of that thing before it decides to give up on its livelihood.'

Mason sat beside Ericka on the concrete barrier alongside the highway. It rested at the edge of the driveway to Ericka's dad's place. It was old, grey like the backdrops in old war films broadcast from Evansville. It showed marks from numerous impacts. Owen was pissing into the tall weeds that grew beyond the hood of the stalled-out, water-logged car they had beached trying to get up the driveway. Ericka nervously hammered the backs of her feet into the face of the barrier. They couldn't hear the tornado sirens up here. The dense trees and the swelling hills hid from their view the town of Wheelerville and the hole bored through its heart, but the image of the sinkhole stuck with Mason, and he had little doubt it was on Ericka's mind as well. Their world was collapsing, for good or ill.

'You figure the state would have picked this thing up?' Mason lobbed a question Ericka's way, hoping to deflect her obvious discomfort. They had been sitting on the barrier for a good ten minutes, the majority of which had been filled with repeated attempts to resurrect Owen's car.

'They would,' Ericka said, 'if they knew it was here. Dad and a couple of his buddies stole it from a road crew in Illinois.'

'Say what?' said Mason. 'These things weigh a ton.'

Ericka shrugged as if explaining simple and well-known facts to a child. Her father could naturally move boulders. 'One of them owns a towing company over in Vincennes. Besides, they ain't so heavy if you got the right way of going about it.' The last line she delivered as if she'd heard the words repeated time and again.

'We could use that tow truck about now,' hollered Owen from the tall grass. He had finished his business and was staring off into the treeline—a not uncommon bit of behaviour that Mason had often witnessed on job sites.

'Why a barrier?' asked Mason.

'Dad has always been a whole lot distrustful of the government.' Ericka was picking at a gouged-out section of the top of the barrier with her left hand. 'Something leftover from being young and hating cops.' She stopped picking and watched a group of starlings swoop between treetops, their movement redolent of the quick puff of dark smoke that follows the first gasps of fire. 'All of them up in Indy was talking about making this road into a state highway. He said it was about the Mexican Free Trade stuff, and that all those truck drivers would be coming up the road hungry and with rape on their minds. We needed some sort of protection.'

Mason was quiet, again unsure how best to respond. Thoughts about the marauding chaos that would be unleashed by the bureaucracy of an inept government ran heavy among the people in this corner of the state. He and Owen had come across this sentiment many times working on the more isolated cell towers in the area. Those who bought into the conspiracy theories and dark worldviews made the real world dangerous. Their type of thinking could cause a lot of trouble for the average guy just trying to clear his work day.

He heard Owen rustling through the tall grass. A squirrel jumped between the branches of some nearby trees. 'What you think about that?' asked Mason.

'I was little,' Ericka said, 'so Dad was always right. Or he meant right by it. But the state never did nothing about this here lump of concrete, nor the road, so I never had to think too deep about it. Plus, it always made it easy to find the place, even in the middle of the night.'

'My worry has got nothing to do with roving bands of libertarian truck drivers,' interjected Owen as he returned to the edge of barrier, 'but whether or not we're high enough up this hillside so as to not have courtside seats to a natural disaster.'

'Dams aren't natural,' corrected Ericka.

'Nope,' said Owen. 'But rain is.'

'He's right,' Mason said. 'We should get moving. Which way is uphill?'

Ericka pointed away from Wheelerville. 'Owensburg is on the other side of that hill. I think about six or eight miles. Soaring Jay Truck Stop over there is the place we get the cheap gas.'

'Should be able to walk that in a couple of hours,' Owen said. He almost sounded happy, as if it were the best part of the day so far.

'You up for it?' Mason asked Ericka.

'Don't think I've got a whole lot of choice,' she replied. 'Doubt my dad's coming back before that flood does.' She was the first of them to turn and begin walking up the side of the road. Mason watched her closely the first few steps. He was certain that her thoughts were somewhere behind her as she moved, uncertain but steady, toward whatever lay ahead.

They arrived at the Soaring Jay Truck Stop at the far end of Owensburg, Indiana, having walked clear over the hilltop and into the next valley. The rain had moved out and the sky had turned over to a deep steel pan. The three of them hadn't seen so much as a distant taillight nor the scurry of a deer back into the woods. They had not spoken much, and Mason was left to his own thoughts, his own voice rolling around his head, which was pretty much filled with thoughts of Ericka.

Ericka had arrived on his front porch just as the place he called home was about to be washed away. The term 'washed away' brought to mind the great flood and the ability of water—from baptism to biblical cataclysm—to cleanse sin and failure. Ericka Knightlinger, her gait steady as she walked the highway a few feet before Mason, became a gift from the divine, an instrument of God to change Mason's world. The life that he had held onto since Meredith had left him in that small town—the collapsed dam, the gal before him, all of his disappointments, all of his hardships—was meant to bring about a change that Mason realized was long overdue.

The parking lot of the service station was full of news trucks from Louisville and Indianapolis, their antennae and satellite dishes thrown up into the sky. The world loved natural disaster stories; everything else was a subplot.

Mason sat on the curb beneath the station's awning, watching as witnesses and outright liars were being shuffled between camera crews and microphones. For some, the torrential rain and the imminently failing dam were disasters of epic proportions. They wept and worried and huddled together in knots of dread. Mason just felt tired. He was damn near exhausted after that hike and his epiphany along it. He took in the scene at the station and decided that what would be, would be. For a guy who'd probably lost all of his earthly goods to a broken dam, he felt the best he had in years. Mason might have ventured to say he felt downright optimistic, if not happy.

One of the big city news crews had corralled Owen in hopes of injecting a little tragedy or drama into their regional weather reports and car dealership ads. Owen was young and handsome in the Southern Indiana blue-collar way, and Mason was sure the crew was reaching for the suburban mom demographic with the interview.

Mason hadn't heard any definitive news that the dam had failed, but he had to assume, given the sheer number of news teams present, that it had. Mason strangely wasn't bothered. He thought of the way that Ericka had kissed him earlier that day in his and Owen's kitchen. He didn't recall much of anything from Dutchey's the night before, but the earlier part of the day came back like sun breaking through the clouds after days of rain.

'Dad is down in New Albany,' Ericka said as she rounded the opposite side of the car. Her voice sounded warm, and welcoming as the approaching evening. 'I used one of the cameramen's satellite phones.' She motioned towards a distant cluster of reporters and news vehicles. The cell towers had failed.

'What's he doing down there?' asked Mason.

Ericka sat down on the bumper beside him. 'He's got friends down there,' she said. 'Sometimes he just bugs out, as he calls it—takes off because he feels the need to. I get the feeling he just needs to get wasted with his buddies.'

'Makes him sound normal,' said Mason.

'Ain't none of us too far different,' said Ericka.

She seemed quiet, tired, and a lot less confident than she had when she had first showed up on his and Owen's front porch. And she looked older, like a day of running from disaster and searching for lost family was enough to snuff out that buzzing energy of pre-grown-up life.

It had, for the most part, stopped raining. Nearby a few errant raindrops collected in a puddle. 'The way everyone is acting here,' said Mason, 'there really ain't gonna be a county to be from.' He knew that stories about hardships rode strong as the reasons that drew his people to this country. Disasters were far from unheard of—tornadoes and closing quarries were all too frequent in Mason's short time on this earth. But he knew this moment was different. This wasn't the classic story of how they came to be Hoosiers from Wheelerville, Indiana. This was about something that was both new and familiar. It was about something else further down the road. It was the reason folks in the lower Midwest listened to Delta blues like it was personal gospel.

'Maybe it's not all bad,' said Ericka.

Mason turned to her.

'The flood, the town, the whole natural disaster thing.' She paused, looked up at him and shrugged. Mason couldn't understand her change in temperament. She'd seemed distant since they'd left her father's trailer, but in that moment, as the rain dissipated and the night stretched on towards morning, Ericka reached out a little, almost touching him. 'How bad would it be if Dutchey's was gone? All the judgy women at the Dollar General, too? They ain't really done me a whole lot of kindness over the years.'

Across the way, Owen was nodding his head to whatever the reporter was saying.

'Guess you could say that about a lot of the town,' offered Mason. He could just about make out the Purple Aces emblem on her shirt in the low light coming off the distant camera equipment. He laughed a little, nudged her knee with his as playfully as he could. All the nervousness that she had carried with her since arriving at his porch disappeared in her smile. It felt like sunlight atop a river on a rainy day.

'So not all of us women are so shitty?' asked Ericka.

'Maybe getting out of the way of Indiana's biggest disaster of the last hundred years is the best way to make sure it's all up from here.' Mason slid closer to her.

Ericka giggled and let out a small uncontrolled snort in response. Mason thought he could see tears welling up in her eyes. She dropped her head down onto his shoulder, leaned her weight against him. She went quiet, taking in the moment, listening absently to the distant prattle of voices in the news crews' scrums. 'What do you suppose Owen is telling them?' asked Ericka.

'Everything and then some,' Mason joked. He was well past his hangover. The air around them was still dense and humid, as if on the verge of a new life. He could feel Ericka breathing calmly against him, and he felt steady, sure and comfortable in a way he hadn't in very long time. 'It's gone, you know?' he said after a few quiet moments.

'Didn't the Lord cleanse the earth with a flood?' replied Mason.

'That's what Reverend Hart says a lot,' she said. Her voice sounded tired. 'My dad says he's a smart son of a bitch.' She paused as the night was momentarily filled with the sound of a passing helicopter. It moved off over the hill in the direction of Wheelerville. 'But the Bible people ain't been too kindly to me or Dad. Don't care if I see them again.'

Mason watched as a charter bus pulled around the bend of the road that led south towards Louisville. The bus was glassy and shone like a skyscraper on a cloudless winter day. It had the cold, lifeless air of the buses that had once brought football teams from Indianapolis to play his high school team. This bus was empty, and he realized that it was there to take them all away to sanctuary while the rest of the world figured out how to put Wheelerville back together. He supposed the media would call them survivors of the flood, maybe even victims, but 'victim' was a word that rang oddly to Mason. No one in that parking lot would have used it in relation to themselves. Every small town in the heartland had no doubt heard the line: it was all about surviving the life afforded by those places. Mason preferred the notion of getting by, of doing whatever it was that made it possible to get through the day.

A few people he recognized from Wheelerville made their way to the open doors of the bus. There weren't enough of them to fill the bus even halfway. Mason hadn't ridden in a coach that nice ever, and wherever it was gonna take him, he wanted to go. 'You won't have to see them again,' he said. 'We won't have to.' Ericka perked up as he spoke. 'Besides, we are well past that one-night thing.' Mason pulled her closer to him. 'Let's get us two seats in that bus. I'm downright sick of walking and waiting. I don't give no rat's ass about trees or cellphone towers, and I'm thinking the two of us could do a whole lot of laying around when we get to wherever the hell we end up. We don't have to be nobody neither of us wants to be.'

Together they stood up and, with his arm still around her thin shoulders, Mason and Ericka boarded the bus. The world they were headed into was no larger than the space around them.

MOTHMAN RETURNS TO MUNCIE

The first time Desmond Hilliard heard tell of the Mothman he was at a University of Evansville seminar for the men's basketball team staff. He, the assistant equipment manager, sat through a talk about dumb luck and sports by an old-timer from up New Castle way.

Mothman had first come to Muncie on January 18, 1972. Phil and Brenda Faust had been coming back from their nephew's basketball game at New Palestine when they saw him. They described him as flapping around above the side of the road, moving like a great blue heron, heading to or away from a lake, and generally looking ominous. The old-timer claimed that seeing the Mothman was a bad omen. Muncie Central had blown a second half lead to New Pal almost two weeks to the day, though Muncie Central had been pegged to win at least divisionals that season. Phil had taken off with Brenda's sister's husband, and just about everyone around town agreed the Mothman's appearance was the real reason for Dobson's Tavern closing up on Jackson Street. Old Man Dobson had until then cooked up the best tenderloin in the surrounding three counties, served the coldest beer and had the lowest prices. The basic conclusion of the talk, if there was just one, was that seeing the Mothman brought about a deep-gouging wave of calamity.

Desmond Hilliard, strange enough, had remembered this talk about a good fifty miles back, near one of the Fisher's exits. He was en route from the interstate to the centre of town—Muncie proper, if you will—when blind misfortune found its way into his world. Through the windshield of his hand-me-down Taurus station wagon, he witnessed a six- to seven-foot-long humanoid gliding between the Dollar

General and the Circle K. Desmond was not shocked by its appearance. He was not scared to see the Mothman for the first time, with its shining eyes, stout head and flaring protrusions of shadow between arms and body. He had seen much scarier-looking creatures in the forests around Brown County. The pedestrians and other drivers did not swerve or stare—their reaction, or lack thereof, suggested that even in broad daylight the Mothman's appearance was, while absurd, far from a cause for terror. He thought of the way the New Castle old-timer had cursed the Mothman, how that man had been convinced that bad luck would befall him.

Desmond, on his way to Central High School to scout for the Wabash College basketball program, flipped off the figure and watched it disappear over a bank of chestnuts and catalpas a couple of hundred yards behind the gas station. This Mothman bullshit had eaten into his time and life in ways he couldn't afford. He had barely a half-hour to grab a burger and some cheap well drinks prior to tip off. He felt doubly pissed that the Mothman had returned to Muncie at the exact moment Desmond set out to scout two AA recruits. It was his big break; those two recruits were pretty damned high on the college athletic director's list.

Given his hard-luck track record, Desmond couldn't help but think that anything could go sour at this point. He hadn't been to Muncie since that old-timer's seminar, and he had looked forward to this particular assignment given the city's reputation as a college town. Desmond believed that Muncie was the sort of place that could change his life—a tempting prospect for a relatively young, single and chronically underachieving basketball scout. Until, of course, the Mothman appeared.

Doris, the stout, large-haired waitress at the Falcon Nest Tavern, had seen the Mothman a solid two weeks before Pence was elected governor. In the days that followed, her dad fell into some intense Bible-thumping revival stuff, spewing brimstone and bullshit to a degree that would make a UHF televangelist blush. Her mother took up pill popping, landing herself in a gay-reprogramming camp as a volunteer counsellor. Doris herself had lost her job at a nearby elementary school for making out with one of the student teachers after consuming a particularly large handful of home-cooked ludes. She blamed the end of manufacturing in her middle-American city on Pence and the damned shadiness of that Mothman.

Desmond explained to Doris, when she brought his second round of well vodka tonics, where in town he had seen the Mothman. She was utterly unimpressed with the details of the encounter. She told him that she wouldn't be looking skyward for at least a good two weeks. She had had enough of that damned Mothman's shit. And as everyone who grew up in Northern Indiana knew, if you don't see shit, there can't be shit. It was how they had dealt with the AIDS crisis in the eighties and how they were currently tackling their problems with homelessness and opioids. This had to be the best way to deal with that fuzzy-winged bastard.

From the Falcon Nest, it was a brisk two-block scramble through deserted streets to make shoot-around at the Muncie Fieldhouse. He walked past mostly empty storefronts and well-swept gutters and tended-to out-of-season planters. The fieldhouse stood opposite downtown, at the edge of one of Muncie's older, now less attractive, neighbourhoods. The short run through the maze of entrances and stairways to the scout and booster section was generally a pleasant affair; however, this time he was haunted with a quiet rage over the Mothman.

Desmond Hilliard was by nature what you might call a hard-luck guy. His day-to-day existence was lived, for the most part, in the quiet between calamities. His mother's people, the only blood relatives he knew, had come from down Brown County way. Not on the touristy Nashville side, more on the Columbus side of things. The Hilliards were just poor enough to be deemed luckless, and just rich enough to avoid being completely miserable. Desmond had grown up through a litany of disasters: burst pipes, deer-crippled cars, that love triangle with Stacey Callister and her cousin Layla Oblack. Layla did smash up his old Honda Civic, and he did drape the contents of a Walmart garbage bin all over her front door. Lots of folks might call that one a calamity. Desmond had learned to brace himself.

Desmond settled into an open seat in a fairly empty part of the fieldhouse a few rows up from Central's bench. Some of the players, mainly the redshirts and a couple of the bench riders, were on the court at shoot-around. Every one of them—except the lanky Latino kid who parked under the basket—was launching three-point shots. These were kids looking to make the biggest impression in a limited amount of time. Desmond's boss, Athletic Director Rory Pritchard, called it the Naismith Anterior Theory, or something like that—the name was one of the little work-related details Desmond often found difficult. He watched as the majority of the shots clunked off the rim—except the ones coming out of the youngest and smallest kid out there. He hit about every fourth shot despite slightly clunky shooting mechanics. It would be years before it would matter, and only if he grew. McDermont. He wrote the kid's name down.

His attention wandered to the hazy vista of hanging lights in the cavernous old gymnasium. It was a classic to these grand middle states, the home to all-American winter nights, the launching point of tri-county AM radio broadcasts, and the orchestral hall for the choral squeak of rubber-soled shoes. This was the rare sign of life in the depths of cold and darkness that would fall upon the state. All of it to be witnessed and heard, from near and far, from the comfort of just around four thousand seats. This was Creation as inherited by Desmond, the place his youthful daydreams had landed him as a mid-thirties adult. Places such as this fieldhouse in Muncie represented the Hickory ambitions shared by generation after generation of Hoosiers, Desmond included.

Some fans, mainly teenagers and their parents, filtered into the stands around him. Desmond's attention drifted from their arrival to the matching series of deep purple championship banners ringing the gymnasium. They were all divisional in nature. Over the years he had often looked up at the banners of high school gyms across the state, pondering—if not full-on dreaming of—what it would be like for even one of those banners to represent his own athletic contribution. Did not contributing in any particularly important manner diminish the success of the individual, the pride, the genuine accomplishment of it all? He considered his teenage self, grade-eleven Desmond, and how he felt when he sat on the second bench in sweats during a championship year. It went against every athletic tenet to think that nothing you did really mattered, that the world around you was determined by more important people. People like the starters for the teams, celebrated at the commencement of each game. The ones who players like McDermont dreamed of becoming despite silently knowing that they never would. He thought about his buddies Tommy Westborne and Julius Reitman, running the fryer at the Dairy Stop, smoking weed and listening to cassettes of underground Louisville hardcore, while he sat and stared and cheered on others. They were all still doing the same shit, himself included, well into their adult years. His gaze came to rest on the 1971 and 1973 banners, then on the thin space between them—the rightful place of honour into which the 1972 pennant should have descended. And it would have, had it not been for the damned Mothman.

Desmond hated the way mythologies had two sides: light and dark, good and evil, winner and loser. He hated that the more pleasant of the two sides so rarely won out in his life. He cursed the Mothman under his breath, something about it being a shiny-eyed motherfucker.

Desmond returned to his notes, but he was interrupted mid-thought by Paige Giamanti, the porcelain-skinned, chiseled-featured scout for the University of Indianapolis. She asked which one of those kids was the motherfucker he was muttering about.

Paige was a predator in the scouting world. She would steal, borrow and manipulate to ensure that her employer got the best results. Like so many fine predators, she was beautiful and sleek and as down-home, girl-next-door as a place like Anderson, Indiana could turn out.

'Wasn't talking about him, actually,' he replied. Her looks won out; Desmond left her an opening for conversation.

'Well, I wasn't liking Norwood's mechanics down there.' Paige motioned to the sophomore standing at the top of the key. 'Watching these bench guys warm up is killing me. Who were you talking about, then? It's got to be more entertaining than what's going on down there.'

Desmond laughed the way that a third-string player did in the presence of the popular girl. He and Paige had become acquainted over the past few seasons. Paige had introduced herself to Desmond at the NCAA media centre during the Sweet Sixteen at the Field-house in Indy a few years back. By nature she was flirtatious with certain fellow scouts, took an interest in the minute aspects of their conversations. She had something his mother would have referred to as hospitality. He liked that word a great deal, sought out its associated traits, but rarely found said traits in others.

'My story's not basketball related,' warned Desmond teasingly.

'Even better,' replied Paige.

Desmond decided to remain as matter-of-fact as possible. He didn't want to get emotional about the cursed Mothman again, or else he would be liable to say something that Paige, with her established reputation as the best basketball scout in Central Indiana, might use to her advantage. Or, he might say something that would make her stop talking to him. He scratched his forehead nervously but let loose with an honesty that he rarely possessed. 'Saw that Mothman on the way into town,' he half-muttered, his voice pitched low as if to admit to his embarrassment.

Paige whistled, shook her head, then returned her gaze to the court below. 'No shit,' she said. 'That asshole is back.'

Paige explained to Desmond, a few hours after the game, that the real problem with the Mothman was the fact that his arrival meant bad shit was about to go down. It didn't always happen the way you imagined it would. You could never be sure if you were going to get walloped by a natural disaster this week or next, or maybe the one after that. Or even if you were the one who was going to get walloped.

Paige Giamanti had seen the Mothman just before one of the biggest games her senior year of high school. She was the all-state lead block for the Anderson Senior girls' volleyball team that year. They should have beat Hartford Senior easily that night, but, in front of scouts from a few states over, they blew an early two-set lead, ended up losing by a good margin in each of the last two. Paige confessed that she had played well enough to impress. But two weeks later, a late-fall twister took out Anderson High's gym. And then she caught her boyfriend sleeping with his teammate from the football team. Things undoubtedly worked out for the better, but the Mothman's appearance had been the catalyst. When the Mothman struck, it knew nothing of grace nor gentleness.

Desmond found the room at the Super 8 smelled too heavily of sex. It bothered him like a summer rainstorm that thickened an already unbearable summer day. He helped Paige's naked legs off his still-naked self. He left the bed and toyed with the fan on the window air conditioner, hoping that fresher air might be found in the parking lot outside. He needed the air to circulate. They had been in the room for the better part of two hours, but he got the sense they were far from finished.

Paige turned on the television and scanned through the channels. The volume was low enough to ride atop the sound of the air conditioner fan. She landed on a station showing plumbers chasing ghosts with tape recorders. When the plumbers caught the ghosts, they began talking to them with flashlights and laser light shows.

Desmond watched her and then the TV for a few moments. He forced himself to play the part of scout. His analytical mind considered player development, future prospects. And his analytical mind turned over her presence, and if he felt a certain shame about it, the feeling was more habitual than heartfelt. Desmond would have to rank Paige a regular blue-chip prospect after this session alone. He could see the former athlete in her. Her body was sleek like a Cold War weapon, smoothly threatening, hardened through action. Her face was a picture of complete seriousness as she took in the onscreen drama.

Desmond walked to the bomb shelter–thick curtains and pulled them open just slightly. It was past dark, and the trees beside the interstate did their best to look intimidating. He always thought that Northern Indiana lacked nature, the raw energy and life of his Southern Indiana home. Everything felt less possible, less probable, north of US 40. Northern life was dictated by the laws of petty township bureaucrats, and every inch of progress seeped toward Muncie as suburban roundabout sprawl. He recalled hearing in his college courses that the dense, dark forests of Indiana were frightening to its first European settlers, that hollers between cabins birthed their Hoosier moniker, that the essence of those forests still haunted each and every resident to this day.

Desmond had grown up exploring some of the state's last mighty forests in Brown County. He had a healthy fear of the wildcats and witches and madmen said to wander the woods. Love for Desmond was one part fear, one part lust. And he loved his Southern Indiana home, loved it for everything it had to be.

He tugged the curtain closed, returned his gaze to Paige, who was lit blue in the glow of the television screen. If there was fear in Muncie, delivered by that wretched Mothman, there was at least lust, too.

He circled the room and returned to the bed. Paige drew him against her as if to remind him that *she* was the celebrated all-star athlete, that life was *her* game. Within her embrace, he felt as if he would still be welcome in the world that made heroes of athletes. It was a comforting thought, and it served to dissipate the sense of impending doom wrought by the reappearance of the Mothman. On the TV, the plumbers were walking around an old theatre in some backwater town, talking about their equipment like big-city hunters with new NRA memberships. They punctuated their patrol with occasional demands that a ghost show itself. The commercial arrived just as a camera man was slammed into the ground by an invisible force.

Paige harangued the plumbers for harassing what they damn well knew was there. They should have known what would happen, like they knew a drain would clog after dumping homemade pickles down it. Anyone with a modicum of intelligence knew that you had to move through the world expecting consequences for certain actions. That you could live in fear or that you could insist that the world, even the unexplained parts, obey your beliefs.

When you ask for trouble, you have to expect it.

Desmond might have forgotten about the Mothman for a good long while, but in a way, it was his ghost. He had wandered into the wrong place at the right moment and he had witnessed its presence. He wasn't wholly sure that Paige was speaking directly to him about any-thing on the television. She sounded reflective, like a scout on a long car ride between gyms, preaching the gospel of basketball as both a religious saviour and a test of will. He considered consequences, said nothing, and ran his free hand down Paige's naked thigh.

The morning didn't start early enough for Desmond. Paige was not, by any measure, an early riser, nor was she a morning person. It was close to ten in the morning before they made their way out of their hotel and to the highway exit Starbucks in a nearby parking lot, a short walk across the rainy grey of the Indiana spring day.

Paige was still taken with the idea that the ghost-hunting plumbers had been harassing the other side. She seemed to have com-pletely forgotten about Desmond's encounter with the Mothman the previous night. He had passing notions of indignation that she had shunned his plight in favour of that of the cable channel ghosts, but they were chased away by the simple fact that she looked good in the backlight of the Starbucks' pastry case. They took up residence at the table furthest from the wall of coffee bean bags, cut into two large red-eyes and breakfast sandwiches that they had ordered out of habit.

Paige moved on to talking about the play of the seniors from Kokomo's boys' team the previous night. She was concerned that they should have been better considering their size and their reputation. The ensuing speech sounded like it might have been delivered by the beloved coach in an inspirational sports movie. She explained that there was a difference between what we expect and what we get; that not all scenarios are best case or worst case; that it's all about worldview and how we execute the plays we're given.

She was halfway through her twenty-eight-ounce coffee and a quarter of the way through her sandwich before she said with admirable directness, 'That's just it with your Mothman.' She proclaimed it—loud enough to be heard by those sitting by the distant shelves of mugs and trinkets—that the Mothman's curse couldn't be all that bad if Desmond had just managed to nail the best piece of ass to come out of Anderson since 2004. It seemed to Desmond that the whole café paused just long enough to assess the validity of that proclamation before falling back into the John Mayer song about questioning the state of Georgia.

A GOLDEN HUE OF EARTH

The thing Miri loved best about Sullivan County summers was the way her skin glowed bronze at the end of a long day on the river. It was July, and even in the air-conditioned depths of Stoney's Tavern, you could feel the heft of the humid air that had descended upon this corner of the heartland. The entire town of Lintonsberry seemed to have gathered in the old bar on Highway 193 across from the banks of the Wabash River. Stoney's Tavern went back at least seven decades and was a backroads combination of a bait shop and a gin joint famous for cold beers and fried fish.

The jukebox was playing Foreigner, just a little too loud. Miriam Fiddler was admiring the remainder of her day on the river in the dim light of the barroom. She swore she hadn't been this tanned since the summer after her graduating year at Lintonsberry Senior, and it made her feel young and strong, a feeling that had been notably absent since she had moved away. The drab skies of Milwaukee had not, in the first month of her vacation, managed to turn her skin back to the glorious golden hue of an Indiana summer. Outside, it was well past dark.

The talk on the river earlier that day, as they coasted down the Wabash, had been of the lighter variety. Stories of acquaintances and relatives, who had been sleeping with who, childhood landmarks and people that had passed into history, and tall tales of mad men and monsters that haunted the forests at the edge of town. Talk that was well suited to the thick haze of cloudless Indiana summer days, lazy and unimportant. Miri wouldn't say that it required a grand expulsion of energy for five or six hours. The river safely guided them from the national forest north of town to the roadhouse on its far south side.

The weather that afternoon had been cruel in all the ways that any Hoosier who knew the place understood it could be. The sky was the yellow-brown of earth denied water. Creation herself had become bathed in a golden hue that painted everything a near sepia in tone. This land was built on visions of an intangible past—a past constructed out of the golden half-life of Gene Stratton-Porter novels, the sweet tea and wilted lettuce of a James Whitcomb Riley porch party, and the impossible reality of lurking violence. Miri, her mind locked in daydreams fostered by Hoosiers long past, had floated between riverbanks. The skin of her arms had grown rosy and warm to the touch. Yet still, it was disturbingly pale, leaving her feeling disconnected from the land and people she had once called home.

'Getting your Indiana summer tan back?' asked Ella. Tall and slender and dark skinned, Ella was the heartthrob of most of the men her age and above in the county. Miri had been friends with her since they were kids throwing hedge balls at the back of the equipment shed at Memorial Park. Ella's older brother had taught Miri how to throw the softball-sized seed pods with weight and speed, to ward off the worst of what the world could and would cast at them.

Ella's brother, Eddie, had been an avid outdoorsman since he could walk. He had seen things and people in the woods around Lintonsberry that led him to encourage his younger sister and her friends to throw shit at a wall in the only park in town rather than play in the woods. It was in no small part what made Ella declare that most of Southern Indiana was full of lurking predators, although that declaration had become a running joke of sorts in recent years. Ella and Miri had never challenged it as neither had spent much time in the woods and farmlands outside of Lintonsberry. The river was fine, due to its constant motion. The Wabash was a pathway through the more menacing portions of the world they all shared. A gentle moving platform from which to observe the untouchable.

'Look out,' said Collins, 'or the sunshine and dirty river will steal you back.'

Collins was also a long-time friend of Miri's. They had known each other since junior high, had circulated in the same group. He had dated one her friends back then, and in the ensuing years after that break-up, was always around when she was, even replacing the long-disappeared friend. He drank and ate too much and seemed to genuinely not give a fuck about his looks nor his direction in life. Not that it mattered; he was handsome enough. He likely would not have been wearing a shirt if it wasn't for Stoney's dress code. He and Ella had relations on occasion.

'I will,' replied Miri. 'It feels good to be back here.' The warmth of her sunburnt skin make her feel like the film of the river was upon her. Her sense was that it was an embrace from the land itself. She was covered in the earth, warmed by its proximity. She knew it would fade like the setting sun, and she clung to it even though her words rang a little hollow for her liking.

'Nothing like the way that Sullivan County makes you feel at home?' asked Ella.

'You could say that,' replied Miri.

The warm embrace of the land had visited her only once before, during those first few days of vacation. It had come when she was walking the distance between her parents' home and the town's Circle K for some fizzy water and snacks. She had felt like a kid in that moment. The feeling had dissipated before she even returned to her parents.

Miri had taken her first job after graduate school at a small liberal arts college library, in a city that wasn't all big and uppity like Chicago and that wasn't Indianapolis. She had found Milwaukee to be as cold and grey as the highways leading up to it. She lived by her work schedule alone, had been on some outings with a new hire in the music department, and she had come to accept the distance between living things and the world she inhabited. Most notable was the coldness of it all.

'Always had you cut out for a city girl,' Collins said. 'You weren't exactly the outdoorsy type. Figured you would like it and we wouldn't be seeing you back here.'

Miri knew that she was seen as the smart one, the reader, one of the few kids in town pegged to go off and do something important in the big city. Her parents had been so resigned to that fate that they were surprised when she announced that she would be taking her two weeks of vacation to head back to Sullivan County.

Miri understood, even if Collins didn't, that his words hinted at the divide between one's home and the place one needed to be. There was a metaphysical severance in a person's life as they grew away from the places they came from and moved into the places they should be. She knew from the way the water and sun had made her feel that this was the land that had nurtured her. The hot, humid day burned on longer and smoother and more beautiful than any day she could remember over the last year, and it made her feel alive in a way that she hadn't since she left. 'It does feel good to be back,' she repeated.

Miri couldn't help but notice how happy she was to return to Lintonsberry, feeling not at all put off by her time away, as if she were stepping right back into all the ways that she would have been if she'd never left. But there was a disconnect that she carried within her. This place was more than sunshine on the river and nice tans in the summertime, but the broth of the river and sun had obfuscated that. The warmth of it all against her skin would fade like it had in the walk to and from the store the other day. She knew it. And in that knowledge, she also had an inkling that there was something to be wary of, something that hid the post-sundown violence and fear that stalked the quieter parts of the state.

James returned to their table. He and Collins had become roommates in Miri's absence. Although long-time friends, James had announced that the reason for their cohabitation was the need to get Collins with more women. Collins had made little of the comment when he explained this to Miri. It was an indictment of the former star point guard from Sullivan Senior High School, the way that Collins hinted that James had not grown into everything that being the teenage town darling had promised. Since her return, Miri had sensed something troubling in James's newfound brooding nature. It was something aggressive, alpha male, and likely one of the aspects of his character that had made him a star athlete. Like the grand big cats on PBS nature documentaries, he seemed to stalk the world, and in return, the world in his presence seemed to be capable of unyielding violence as well as compliancy bordering on a waking coma. James deposited a half-finished beer onto the table, leaned over it like a predator exhausted from the hunt but still hungry.

'What?' asked Collins. 'No woman draped over your arm?' James had left the table almost fifteen minutes prior, his gaze locked on one of the Rizzo girls from upcountry.

'Nah,' replied James. 'She's into it. But not ready yet.' He sat down hard in an empty chair beside Miri and scanned the table for a visible response to his bravado. 'I'm just laying the groundwork.'

'Whatever you want to call it,' said Ella. She shook her head.

James sneered in response, like a panther before striking. He had said very little to Miri throughout most of the day and had acted somewhere between shy and boastful to the others. He had been visibly unnerved by her return, as evidenced by his brooding quiet. It was nothing that a few beers hadn't managed to unwind since they had arrived at Stoney's. He slapped his arm around the back of Miri's chair with a dramatic exhale. 'But what about our Miri?'

She glared back at James, partially in confusion, partially in defiance. His tone was mocking, if not downright demeaning. She looked him in his wild, forest-green eyes. 'What about me, James?' She had kept her distance from him out a general dislike for the man, and she felt uncomfortable and annoyed by his attention. He stank from having consumed at least three beers too many.

'Maybe I would just like to hear your wit,' James replied with a hungry smile. A predatory glint kicked up in his eyes. It stoked the heat of her discomfort. She recoiled, felt herself bunching up, drawing inward and leaning away from James's arm. 'I eat that brainy shit right up,' he boasted.

'Yeah,' said Ella, 'because wit and brainy stuff is how we all measure each other around here. You're still riding with us, aren't you?' There was an edge to the way she said it, as if she meant the comment to pull attention back to her.

'Those community college courses of yours are really paying off,' replied James. 'You got one semester there and now you are making like you are the one that gets to call people stupid.'

Even without the college courses, it was pretty clear that James Vaughn was hardly smart enough to finish high school without a little help from the athletic director's sway. He was uniquely James Vaughn, perhaps best defined by his still-present six-pack, chiseled jawline and bouts of rage, but he was also decidedly familiar.

For Miri, Lintonsberry and her childhood visions of Indiana consisted of sun-warmed skin and a light-headed wooziness, and Friday night fish frys after a day on the Wabash. It was defined by the warmth of summer sunshine and the proximity of unmanageable men. Alarmingly, but not entirely unexpectedly, she could sense a dark hunger in James; he had become one of those unmanageable men.

But it was worse than that. He had within him the sort of hunger that was generally contained in the wilderness of the forests beyond town. Maybe that wild streak had always been there in him, but it had grown in her absence, like weed trees consuming an abandoned farm, destroying the fertility of a fallow field. In such bramble, the uncontrolled nature of the animalistic human surfaced with an unyielding hunger and uncertain anger. This was the spirit that existed in the dark hollows of the thick Southern Indiana forests, forests that predated the axes and fires that European settlers wielded to fight that sort of wildness. Like those settlers, she didn't know why it was there, nor how it had begun to bubble to the surface, but as often happens with the approach of dangerous storms, Miri sensed in her bones, in the twitch of her muscles, in the pressure in the very back of her head, that there was something evil afoot. She dared not oppose it; instead she chose to huddle up against its approach.

James slammed his beer bottle into the table. Stoney's was loud enough to muffle the crash, but all three of his tablemates paused in shock. Miri held her breath momentarily and dared not move with his arm still positioned around the back of her chair. Ella turned her defiant gaze from him to the bottle. James let out an alcohol-fuelled laugh. 'Joke,' he proclaimed.

'Man,' said Collins after an uncomfortable break, 'I still like me some high school livin'. Sure as shit beats driving a truck.'

'When you drive a truck,' prodded Ella. Her voice as she spoke to Collins carried all the familiarity between them that Miri would describe as tenderness. James noticed it too. It appeared to make him more uncomfortable.

'Part-time is enough time for me,' answered Collins. 'Delivering cabbage to Terre Haute and Danville ain't something we need to be doing daily.'

'Collins,' Miri said, 'you haven't changed a bit.' She shifted her stance forward, almost leaning into the table. She had always enjoyed his carefree way of living. He drifted between groups of friends, and as long as she could remember, he kept no long- nor medium-term affairs with women, though he often encouraged them in others. Collins seemed to sweat a sense of detachment that made him all the more alluring as a friend, something of a prize, unique. He was comfortable in his detached way, yet it had been he who had remained loyal to James. Something about their friendship she didn't understand, a loyalty built out of an unreadable past and a drive to maintain that past, however uncomfortably, in the present.

'You didn't answer me,' James said. He ran his fingertips along her shoulders. 'How does old Lintonsberry hold up to life in the big city?' The way he said it, she knew he was probing for something. His cadence, his touch alarmed her. She could sense her own emotions mirrored in the reactions of both Collins and Ella. Their faces held no shock, but rather annoyance and growing discomfort.

'I've always liked Jim Nabors singing at the Indy 500,' she

answered. Ella and Collins laughed along with her. James smiled and pulled back. He had not gotten what he wanted. He seemed to know he wasn't going to be getting it. Miri excused herself from the table and headed to the bathroom. James had unnerved her. The back of her left knee ached on account of the approaching storm.

The restrooms at Stoney's were past the bar in the long, straight hallway that lead to the back door and the parking lot beyond. Miri wove through the tables with tunnel vision that kept at a hazy distance the large number of people gathered in the small tavern. Some of the patrons she vaguely recognized; others were familiar like trees along Route 63. Old, ratty, almost forgotten hand-written posters and flyers on the bathroom walls gave the already dim space a darker air. It made her recall the light, sinister sensation of James's fingertips against her skin. It was lonely and evil and enveloping like a county fair carnival three seasons past its close.

As she waited to use one of the two stalls, Miri overheard two older women talking about the mythic big cats of the Southern Indiana hill country. The huskier of the two said that she hadn't seen one in her whole life, nor had her mother's people. The beanpole with dirty mop-water hair laughed at her friend, reminded her that no one in her own family been out past sundown more than five times in the last half-century, and that cats only prowl at night. That's why people like her could go on thinking there weren't any of them around.

Miri recalled the wildcat rescue she had visited a couple of times in high school. There were definitely big cats in Indiana, real cougars and tigers and lions. But to the best of any Hoosier's knowledge, all those cats were safely behind fences and netting. Indiana had a way of hiding the worst things that stalked creation. These same Hoosiers also tended to fall asleep not long after sundown.

She washed her face in cold tap water and felt the dried salty sweat run off of her. The muted calm of the restroom gave way to the clatter of dishes, the rush of voices and the heat of the packed interior of the tavern. Wait staff rushed past her in each direction. She excused herself as she passed too closely to a few older men heading in the opposite direction. Miri swore that Stoney's had gotten a lot busier during her quick trip to the restroom. The single room felt smaller, shrinking even more as she dodged errant bodies. The wide-open freedom of her afternoon on the river ran dry before her. The once comfortable heat of the place took a turn towards smothering. By the time she arrived back at the table she was downright uncomfortable, a sentiment she knew she wore very clearly on her face.

Upon her return to the table, Miri found James in the middle of a passionate revelation of some great injustice. He mentioned a name that Miri sort of recognized as the person from whom he learned all the 'truths' of the world. Ella gave Miri a look that showed she recognized the discomfort of her friend but did not want to bring undue attention to it. Collins had been following James's story with a smile that said he was equally uncomfortable with what was being served. 'What's the story?' she asked.

'Oh!' Ella jumped at the interruption. 'James was just telling us about one of his fan boy moments with his favourite radio show people.' James shook his head at Ella's commentary and stopped telling the story.

'Don't tell me you're hooked on talk radio?' asked Miri. She knew talk radio to be the bane of life in rural Indiana. It was among the worst of the addictions inherited by working men and, very occasionally, women in the area. The vitriol of corporate-sponsored radio hosts filled the gaps left behind by the dying belief in paycheque evangelists. The hosts spent their time peddling panacea drugs and used the rhetoric of underachieving men to assure listeners they were hard done by in this life through no fault of their own. This was the religion that sprouted in the parts of the world that were ignored by successful, monied people. It was a religion that bred in the darkness between radios, in the quiet of long miles between work and home, and in the emptiness and resentment caused by being underpaid at absolutely every job offered to you.

'Hooked?' scoffed James. 'I like what I like. So I listen to those talk radio shows.' There was raw hostility in his voice, directed primarily at Miri. She knew better than to press it. She sensed that his heroes may have been preaching about big city women and the wrongs they had committed in the recent past. James's focused anger added to the weight of the room. Miri tried not to roll her eyes, but they must have let slip. James shifted his weight forward, as if ready to pounce. 'You don't like my listening choices?'

'Your time,' she replied, 'your choice.' Miri peered at the windowless steel door that lead out of Stoney's. She was mapping her exit. James was a tempest building in the small room. Too many beers and a failed flirtation with the server (whom Miri vaguely recognized as the little sister of someone she knew) had left a wounded predator. The pleasantness of the warm Indiana day had given way to the night, and to the dangerous creatures that lurked in the shadows between trees and highway interchanges and strip malls.

Miri excused herself abruptly and headed out into the night. She was intent on getting away from this heaviness inside of Stoney's, even if it meant walking back to town alone. Wandering around in the dark in places like Lintonsberry was definitely an abnormality. Though she'd been away a short while, Miri was accustomed to the rhythms of Southern Indiana. Night was nothing to be afraid of, she told herself. She had, in fact, walked the road several times over the years, a good number of those alone, although as far she could recall, her walks always took place in daylight. But the night as it was was better than the trouble brewing at Stoney's. It was only about a half an hour's worth of walking, and the night air was cooler than it had been for the last week or so—so much so that the weather was almost inviting. Miri fished out her cellphone and fired off a quick text to Ella explaining that she needed to walk off the night's indulgences.

She headed through the hard-packed gravel of Stoney's parking lot and onto the broad, grassy shoulder that ran along the road back into town. Well outside, the sound of muffled songs emanated from the roadhouse. The night responded with an eruption of tree frogs and the cries of cicadas. As her senses filled with that serenade, and with the darkness away from the lights and the jukebox racket of Stoney's, Miri became immersed in the whirr of the Indiana night. Creation was loud, alive and full of the pride of being. She thought of the two women in the bathroom, their talk about not going out past dark and their willful disbelief in the unseen parts of creation. There were parts of Indiana, great portions of Sullivan County, that she had not wished to see nor remember when she was away.

The sound of the land at full raucous volume, the white noise with which summer nights moved, was one of those things that she had forgotten. It was quieter in Milwaukee—even with the cars and traffic and factories—and the night air was less alive. Miri had taken to night walks in her urban Milwaukee neighbourhood. She was not sure that she had been looking for something that had been absent. Perhaps it was the living, breathing edge of creation. Something that her youth and her relations hinted were most present in the absence of daylight. She had not found it in the streets of her big city neighbourhood.

She had been walking for about five minutes when she spotted movement in the tall grass across the road. Miri slowed. Her intuition told her that some creature had emerged from the river below. She noticed a pooling of water, a vibration of cattails, and then, between two groups of parted reeds, she saw it standing there, across the road and slightly north of her. She understood all at once that this was not her land and that it never had been.

The animal, the cat, stood in the tall grass between Miri and the river below. She made out its form in the passing lights of a half-tonne. Its eyes burned reflective neon before shimmering into a golden hue of sun-baked earth. Its body, too, was a light golden colour, with fur that was glossy, heavy and dark with water from the Wabash. Their gazes met, and Miri instantly understood this creature to be significantly larger than her, but she felt no alarm at its presence. There was a disappointment in its eyes, like the last thing it wanted was to be known, discovered. As the heat of the night mixed with the cat's fixed gaze, Miri sensed that she was far from safe, that it was not necessarily this night-time apparition but what she didn't see, didn't fully understand as being possible, that could hurt her—or worse.

She felt the buzz of her phone as several messages poured through. The lights and roaring sirens of an Indiana state trooper's car ripped open the night. A flurry of dirt and a cacophony of metal flung by her. She glanced back at the cat to find swaying cattails and a small puddle where it once stood. She lingered for a moment, retrieved her phone.

> Ella: James got strange. 11:23
>
> Ella: We will pick you up. 11:26

It was now 11:33. Miri ran to follow the state trooper's lights. The sounds of tree frogs drowned out the crunch of her sneakers biting into the gravel of the shoulder.

When she hit the edge of the parking lot, she saw James face down on the ground with a state trooper's knee in his back. To the side was the Rizzo girl, visibly upset, with the other officer beside her. Behind them, Collins and Ella were waiting by the door, Ella glancing anxiously around the lot. Miri texted her, *meet you at Collins's car.*

Miri stalked around the troopers, moving with the knowledge that the last thing she wanted was to be seen.

BLACKFORD COUNTY LIGHTS

After dark, the world between Kokomo and Hartford City became a glowing archipelago. Each streetlight cast an island of light from crooked utility poles strung loosely with electric lines. Beyond lay a void of night-ordained darkness peppered with stars and the occasional determined blinking of distant aircraft lights. It had been like this for as long as Lucas could remember. Driving between work and home across the serving platter of land that was bisected by the two-lane highway took about an hour or so, but the commute was less monotonous than his time on the line at Midland Automotive. The comparison would be harder to maintain now that he had his layoff notice in hand.

Lucas Hatton and George Fox were driving home post-shift without much in the way of conversation. They had split driving duties over the past few months since they had always managed to find themselves on the same shift—and with the same need to save a few extra bucks. They needed to pay for all the things that life told them they required, even though life also refused to pay enough for them to afford them.

The edge of an envelope fluttered from the force of the dashboard air conditioner. Their near-identical indefinite layoff letters were, in large part, to thank for that quiet. The layoff notices had come without fanfare or official discussion from management, but both men could and should have guessed at their imminent arrival. News stories about recessions and global trade pacts filled the airwaves during their two hours' worth of daily commuting. George Strait and outlaw country gave way to corporate news—their staple background music over the year or so they had been carpooling.

Neither had said much during the previous thirty miles of their transit. They said nothing at all when the newsman highlighted the indefinite layoffs issued at Midland Automotive.

'Suppose Kate and the kids know now,' said George. He was three years younger than Lucas, forty pounds heavier, and blissfully content with the poverty afforded by four kids and a stay-at-home wife.

'You think they are up and listening to the radio?' asked Lucas. He doubted his own wife, Jenny, would have been awake to hear the news. They lived two practically separate lives. Though married five years now, they barely saw each other, let alone talked. It explained their lack of children, though he did not share that explanation with others.

George laughed. 'Yeah,' he said, 'Kate stays up as late as she can. And you gotta know that the news is on damned near every channel.' Two news segments later, George explained to Lucas how he'd been laid off from jobs before; how his dad had been laid off many times over the course of his decades of work; how his grandfather and all of Kate's family had experienced layoffs firsthand; how it was just part and parcel of being a Blackford County man. Wasn't nothing to get worked up over. Family life gives you the long arc of things.

Lucas could feel a talk about kids coming on, about why he didn't have any. About how they can make all the bumps, like unemployment, more bearable. But George stopped himself, as if understanding the reception he would get. It wouldn't have been the first time those sorts of words were said between them. But in this moment, likely their last drive back from Kokomo together, it felt played out. Both men seemed to understand, as if by instinct, the checklist of items that would follow: kids made life's bumps bearable; unemployment was as fleeting as parenthood wasn't; there was pride to be had in witnessing them do the completely possible. Instead they listened to the next Charlie Pride song, and then the Mel Tillis one that followed, before speaking again.

They were about thirty minutes or so from Hartford City, just crossing the opposite side of Gas City, before George spoke.

'What you figure you'll do with yourself tomorrow?' he asked.

Lucas hadn't thought much about it. He would likely sleep late like he always did. Wait around till Jenny got back from work. He knew the anxiety would fly then, so he stopped himself short of too much planning. What the hell would he say to her? They shared a bank account, but outside of that, could he really anticipate Jenny's response to his unemployment? He knew more about drop vinyl on car seat moulds than he did about what his own wife might say about him losing his job. He felt terrible, like a Johnny Cash song. 'Sleep in,' he said simply. 'Maybe spend some time with Jenny.'

They passed the next few moments in silence. The dark blur of the Northern Indiana countryside slipped by until the end of the second refrain of an Alabama song. Lucas watched as a triangular cluster of bright lights flooded a nearby bank of trees with a blinding white glow. The lights emanated from a huge, hovering object that was larger even than the copse over which it had appeared. It slowly rose into the sky until it hovered at least double the height of the Gas City water tower. The object was less than a half-mile away and was defiantly closing the distance between them. The radio crackled, the speakers throwing out static as if the station had chosen to broadcast the cries of trillions of lonely, distant stars. Lucas slowed the car. The road was empty except for them and had been for the last fifteen minutes.

'The fuck is that?' exclaimed George.

Lucas said nothing. He knew what he believed it to be, but hesitated to voice it, as if to name the apparition was to confirm its presence. Aliens and their mysterious ships were commonly held mythologies in his circle. These stories were of the sort one trotted out on hot summer nights over drunken bonfires, or on front porch swings. Thing was, their lives were generally very real affairs, with work and mortgages, and now unemployment and uncertainty. Mythologies were escapes, release valves to let off the pressure of those hard, almost uncontainable parts of life. Lucas was ready, had always been ready, to deal with these mythologies as his relations and neighbours had showed him: by burying them deep, alongside childhood trauma and the full-body ache that came from years of manufacturing labour. He could explain being laid off to others. But seeing—and believing in—giant UFOs in the Indiana night would be too much. A tinfoil hat was just one more cross Lucas was unwilling to bear.

The car lights cut out. The engine sputtered to a halt. They drifted.

'You didn't turn the car off, right?' asked George. He was attempting to maintain the control that Lucas had come to expect of him, but his voice was rattled.

Lucas shook his head. He couldn't reply. His attention was fully occupied by the closing object, the sheer immensity of it. It moved, quiet-like, deliberately, inexorably approaching. It was at least as large as the Midland Automotive back in Kokomo. He glided the car to a stop on the shoulder of the road.

'Dead,' mumbled Lucas. His eyes were fixed on the skin of the ship before them. It was reflective, smooth and dark as the stretches of sky between stars. It closed the distance between them at the speed of quick-drift clouds.

'I mean you kind of knew it,' George said, 'but holy shit, you never really expected to *know* it.' He reached over and shut off the radio. The world went silent.

Lucas still stared at the skin of the ship. The craft was wholly independent of everything around it and below it. He recalled sitting on the banks of Lake Monroe, at the cabin that he had rented with Jenny, looking up at the stars and sky. The ship moved through the air like the clouds had those nights at the cabin. Lucas had thought, then, that the clouds helped to anchor him to the ground, that they contained something of the world beneath him, reminded him that his place was on the grass beside Jenny. But the ship before him now was nothing of that magnitude. Its body was an extension of the endless sky above. The mere presence of it engulfed his anchor to creation. He felt lost in its massiveness. He was crushed by the way its appearance negated the comfort he took in the reality he had come to accept.

'Thinking we should just wait it out,' George stammered. 'Abductions and cow mutilations and whatnot.'

'Whatnot?' replied Lucas. 'You know the talk?'

'You do, too,' said George.

Lucas nodded. He did know the talk. He had spent years listening to Art Bell, the great truth speaker of the high desert, during overnight shifts at the Flying J. Every hour-long block of the show helped him measure when he could leave and stop staring down customers. He knew he should be somewhere else. The show would end as the return of the morning suffocated the last of the night's darkness. The final bars of the outro would signal the approach of a fiery dawn horizon, prodded into being by the day to come. He would arrive back home in Hartford City, at the Harrison Street bungalow he shared with Jenny, moved but never transformed. Jenny would wait for him in the cool comfort of home, lulling him to sleep after a long, sultry summer night.

'I could never listen to Rush,' offered George, 'because they made me think of UFOs.' He spoke with the confessional tone of a man who believed his final words were near. 'You know, nightmares and shit.'

'I don't know,' answered Lucas. 'But I also wouldn't listen to Rush.'

The ship lingered over the bean field before them. There was no exhaust from the ship, no sound, not the slightest indication beyond their eyes and their stalled-out car, that would tell them it was actually there. *Were these arcane craft always here?* Lucas wondered to himself. Rumours and tall tales about UFOs didn't just come from syndicated talk radio hosts. They came from his grandparents and his parents and most of his cousins. Lucas wondered if extraterrestrial ships were nothing more unusual than whooping cranes. Had those aliens—he hated using that word—always existed here, unseen, choosing only now to appear to him? Maybe it was God. Everything was God, after all, or it was supposed to be God. Jenny would have said that. 'Gotta figure God sent it to us,' he blurted out.

'Say what?' asked George.

'God,' he answered. 'These things been around. Only special people get to see them.'

'Special?' snapped George. 'They kidnap people, haunt them every day after. Those things ain't no plan of God's.'

But Lucas knew that, whatever the ship was, it was a gift from God, a clear answer to his woes. Here was his way out of the revolving door of unemployment and depression and loneliness. If he ended up a Hoosier Travis Walton, he wouldn't care about not earning a paycheque from putting vinyl car seats together. After three years of overnight shifts at a trucker gas bar, bathed in nearly a thousand gospels of how his working-class Hoosier life would unfold, he understood that a gift from God had the power to transform you, even into what you could no longer be. Lucas Hatton was no longer a factory worker. But he was still a man who followed God, who thought way too much about the wife he feared he no longer really knew, and who was willing to accept any way out of the path that lay ahead of him if he stayed in Hartford City.

'That's the thing with the Lord,' answered Lucas. 'We are all too dumb to see much of any plan. We just gotta have a little courage … or a lot of courage when something new breaks the surface.'

'Surface?' George said. There was rising alarm in his voice. 'That thing is bigger than the Hoosier Dome and floating down from the sky. What the hell are you talking about faith for?'

'Faith,' Lucas repeated. He liked the way the word sounded when he spoke it. 'I'm thinking I'll get a closer look at this whole "God's plan" thing. Tell Jenny I'm just taking care of a couple of things before I get home.'

'Wait, what?' demanded George. Lucas could hear the worst parts of the *2112* album in his voice. He had always hated Geddy Lee's voice.

Lucas unbuckled his seatbelt and threw open the car door in one swift motion. George was frozen in terror. Lucas exited the car and walked across the embankment between the road and the farm field. He looked down, took great caution with his footing, keeping the better part of his vision on the skin of the craft. The ship began to rotate in place, spinning at a steady pace as he walked towards it. He was certain that whatever was inside was watching his approach. He made his way to the field and stood dead centre below the craft. It filled the sky above him totally, blotting out stars and passing aircraft, reflecting trees and grasses. The skin contained ribbons of glowing, dim lights. Lucas followed them as they rotated around him and felt as if he were the centre of all existence, as if the universe itself rotated around him, as if all that mattered was what he could envision. Lucas was lost in the rotation, had been standing still for what felt like a long while. The world around him flooded with light the colour and heat of gas station canopy lights. Though he listened, he could hear nothing beyond the ringing in his ears.

Lucas awoke in a bean field seventeen miles outside of Hartford City, Indiana, in the darkness of a very early morning. The wind pushed through the leaves of the nearby bean plants. He was sprawled on his back atop a row of them. He felt well rested, as if he had just woken from a quick nap. The sky above him was massive and full of dimming stars.

He got to his feet, perplexed by his loss of time and the lingering memory of the impossibly real UFO, but mostly perplexed by the tranquility of the world around him. In the distance he heard a few bars of the outro from *Coast to Coast AM*—synth-pop to greet the emerging day. He turned to the road and saw his car, both doors open, headlights off. George nowhere to be found. A torrent of disappointment flooded over him.

THE ETCH A SKETCH SHAMAN

'This guy does all this with old cassette tapes?' asked Jessamyn. She hovered an outstretched index finger a few inches from the picture hanging before her. She was pointing at Tom Waits in an all-too-familiar pose on a crème-coloured canvas. His outline was dark and shiny, like the leading edge of an oil spill.

'He does,' replied Trevor. He stood directly beside Jessamyn, closely examining the next canvas in line: a reproduction of Frank Zappa in his younger years, silhouetted on a mint-green background. Zappa was majestic in stature. Trevor, in his late twenties with a mustache and a mop of thick, shaggy hair, attempted to match the posture before slumping back into his comfortable farm-boy slouch. Trevor's stance and form were modelled more after Vonnegut, hinting at humility and quiet self confidence. 'He was working on a couple pieces when I was over at his place a few weeks back,' said Trevor. 'He uses old cassettes someone traded him for a couple of old car speakers at the booth he runs at the flea market over Irvington way.'

Trevor had initially described Edgar Moore as that one great hustler artist that every Midwestern city should, and generally does, manage to develop. Trevor knew him in the way that small-town friends often knew each other, in a sort of life-out-of-time fashion that knew no beginning and no end.

Jessamyn was a little taller than Trevor, a year younger, and she carried the dark hair and tanned complexion of her Persian father with the fine, angular features of her mother. She was a newcomer to Indianapolis and had met Trevor a few months ago at a Pacer's game during an event held by the pharmaceutical company she worked for.

Now, a mere few weeks into her new job in the research lab position, she realized her one single and 'hip' friend actually from the Circle City was Trevor. He was a bona fide Hoosier and good company in the way very few other men or women at work managed to be. She might have called this particular night a date, seeing as it was only her and Trevor. The two were awkward together and quite comfortable at the same time, but there was an emotional and physical line that neither one had been willing to cross.

Jessamyn wiggled her finger, undertook a deeper, more considered assessment of the picture, then dropped a step back to take in the rest of the canvases that hung on the wall of the makeshift gallery. There were a good ten or eleven, all the same size. It was fairly mundane folk art, but there was something near magical in the way it struck her.

'He sounds like a flea market professional,' she opined. She realized that she sounded like a judgy out-of-towner and quickly added sympathetically, 'The things we do to get by.'

'He works that booth in the flea market,' offered Trevor, 'but he's a little better known as an artist. A shamanic artist—a healer of sorts. Like the Lenape kind we stole the state from. He used to be pretty famous about it.'

Jessamyn hummed in reply. The idea of a shamanic artist fascinated her. Back home, Indiana was often referred to as a backwoods kind of place, full of farmers, conservatives and religious zealots. Out of something that was undoubtedly not a coincidence, Toledo's local Bible-thumping television station ads featured a majority of Indiana P.O. boxes. There was something evangelical about the land she had come to inhabit. A lot of her neighbours had seemingly bought into it, for good or ill. The daughter of Muslim auto workers, she had an undergraduate degree in microbiology, but she was curious and wanting when it came to spirituality in America. Edgar Moore, the shamanic healer-artist, was about as interesting as it got for Jessamyn.

Trevor texted her three days later, midweek, over her lunch break. She was sitting in her car, eating a take-out salad from a deli located between her lab and the freeway. She read between bites.

> Trevor: Edgar invited me and you to his studio tonight
> Trevor: working on spectacular new project
>
> time? where?
>
> Trevor: 8. will pick you up

Jessamyn thought about it. A night out on a work night. It wasn't something she had done since her university days. She mused over the thought with another bite of lettuce and onion and then considered a full verse and chorus of the Rolling Stones singing about shining a light. She had found the Zappa cassette canvas interesting enough. And the way Trevor had hinted at the story of the Etch A Sketch salvation ... it all interested her beyond anything she could watch at home on Netflix. Although she knew, too, that going out with Trevor and any of his artist friends left her in a bad way for sleep. It was only Wednesday, and Thursday would seem an entire winter away from the weekend. She quelled that thought. She should damn well have had enough sleep in her life. This was a once-in-a-lifetime chance to meet an artist-shaman.

> K. Be ready after 7:30.

She didn't want to sound too eager to get out, but she had heard stories of the awe inspired by these great healers of men. And awe was a state Jessamyn had for a long time been looking to achieve. One of her more devout aunts claimed to have seen a mixed Miami-Persian healer cure an entire lead-contaminated neighbourhood with a seventy-five-year-old turkey wing and the hood ornament off a Hudson pickup truck. She said the artifact shimmered in every light and that the feathers twitched in the slightest breath. Her aunt's conviction had made Jessamyn undyingly curious to see this shamanic practice or something like it.

Her parents and siblings, adherents to the rational industrialism of the upper Midwest, thought such notions of the extraordinary were ridiculous, and they often said so. They also had opinions of nearby Indiana. Hoosiers were well known to be old-timey, rooted-in-the-dirt people whose understanding of the land and of the divine came from living so close to the earth. Her parents and siblings called them rednecks and hicks—appellations that without a doubt came from their need to acclimatize to their new part of the world, to internalize well-rooted prejudices.

But for Jessamyn, a shamanic artist was just the sort of person who would bring her closer not only to that sense of awe she craved, but also to an understanding of what inspired it.

―――――――――――

It was significantly past sundown when Jessamyn and Trevor rolled down the cracked pavement of Pleasant Street, driving slow through the poorly lit, heavily tree-lined streets that connected the clustered shotgun houses of the Fountain Square neighbourhood to the rest of Indianapolis. Parking was a true commodity in the neighbourhood, and it took a solid few passes around the block before they found a spot. They traipsed the distance of a long city block to get back to the house, saying little, as was often the case with the two of them. Jessamyn was taken in by the pastoral quiet of the neighbourhood. She heard the wind through the trees, the chatter of an occasional television or radio from inside the homes. And although the street was clearly poorer and more ramshackle than many of the city's destination neighbourhoods, she felt well at ease walking through the scantily lit streets.

Trevor led them through a chain-link fenced yard to the front steps of a brown and red shotgun house. Unlike some of the newer homes in the slowly gentrifying neighbourhood, this particular house still had a wood porch. The greyish wood poked though in patches beneath the chipped-away paint, and it was surprisingly sturdy underfoot. The boards did not creak when they walked across them. They came to the door and Jessamyn could make out classic country emerging from behind it. The song was something upbeat in that strange way the saddest country songs often were. Trevor took a moment to warn her that, as far as he could tell from his afternoon run-in with Edgar at Peppy Grill, the man was in his high creative mode. Either this was a gentle caution that the man might be a little less than personable, or it was a more dire warning, akin to a sign at the zoo: The tigers are ornery today. Jessamyn could tell Trevor was slightly concerned about his friend's state based on the way he waited for her head to nod in understanding before he turned and knocked on the door.

'A little quirkiness just adds to the whole experience,' she said in the tense few moments between unanswered knocks. 'And I do love quirky.'

Before Trevor could complete his third knock, the door opened, unhurriedly enough, without the heavy sound of a disengaging lock. A rather tall, long-haired and bearded middle-aged man stood in the open frame, wearing boxer shorts and a loose-fitting kimono. The pattern on the kimono depicted trees and tulips and vintage race cars. The country music, decidedly Nashville in nature, rushed out into the street past the man's mostly naked form. His chest, belly and legs were tanned like a farm worker's and covered in splotches of paint. A heavy smell of cannabis snuck out behind the wall of country music.

'Trevor,' he said in a partially controlled burst of joy. He reached out and enveloped Trevor in a hug, complete with one hand on the back of Trevor's head. His embrace was like that of the sweetest imam Jessamyn had ever known. 'You're here right when you need to be,' said Edgar. He caught sight of Jessamyn standing behind. 'You must be Trevor's friend?' he asked, remaining in the embrace with Trevor for a moment or two longer.

'I am,' she answered. She recited her name and considered

offering a handshake but settled on a half-wave. Edgar nodded at her and then released Trevor.

'Trevor's friend,' he replied. 'From?'

'Well, I have a place in Little Flower now,' she answered, 'but I'm from Toledo.'

'Jessamyn from Little Flower, it is a pleasure to meet you.'

Inside the house was a series of thin, deep rooms, freshly painted in an off-white, and all clean and orderly. They walked into what was surely the living room as it featured a couch and a few plush chairs, all of them looking decidedly second-hand. Towards the back of the room sat an older, comfortably worn man with well-pressed jeans, a fine farmhand-inspired checkered shirt, and a smoke in between his fingers. He lounged in a plush recliner beside a record player and a large vintage stereo. He threw off a look that was far from inquisitive; he was in a seemingly meditative state, fully immersed in the lyrics of the old country song pouring out of the stereo.

'That's my dad,' offered Edgar. He picked up an already opened water bottle and took a swig from it.

The old man in the chair nodded, offered a right-hand salute to the new arrivals. Edgar explained that his dad had stopped by after a few games of chess with his buddies at the nearby diner, Peppy Grill. His father had taken up the essential role of playing the records while Edgar worked on his newest and most significant piece yet. Music was everything, and keeping it going was likely the most important task of the entire evening. Edgar declared that it was a rare treat to get Hector out this late on a school night. Hector said nothing, simply lit his cigarette and stood up to flip the record over when the song ended. He glanced at his son before returning to his chair in the brief hiss before the music started up again.

Edgar led Jessamyn and Trevor into the room that should have been the dining room. Strains of music poured out of the living room and followed them—an anthem to the beauty of a coal mining town somewhere down near the Ohio River. The song was all about hard work and the guilty romance of long-time shift work, low pay and cold beer. The words and the sounds of the guitars were tough in the way most Americans from the southern heartland imagined themselves to be. Even in its relative unfamiliarity, Jessamyn found an agreeable melody with which to hum along. She looked back at Hector. They shared a glance—his a rueful 'welcome to my world'. Edgar, Jessamyn and Trevor stopped before a cluster of work surfaces.

She lingered over the materials spread out and in piles on the tables. There were several pieces of canvas with what looked like fur adhered to them. The canvas was loose, as if it were part of a costume. There were paint cans, too, bearing logos that looked both corporate and familiar, though not quite familiar enough to unearth a clear memory.

'Trevor tells me you like that Zappa I did.' He spoke directly at her.

'I did, I did,' replied Jessamyn. 'You made his moustache the perfect sort of shiny.'

Trevor laughed.

Edgar nodded, followed Jessamyn around the table. He made no move nor sound to explain anything she examined. When they reached the halfway point, he suggested that Zappa was a healer of sorts who used the dissonance between what people thought music should be and what it actually was to pull the healing medicine out of the universe. 'I once told Hector that Zappa's mustache was a metaphysical antenna, well tuned for receiving the gospels of Creation.'

'He said them exact words,' shouted his father from the other room.

Unsure how to respond, Jessamyn nodded and launched a broad smile back at him. She returned her gaze to the table. 'New project?' Jessamyn asked.

'New project,' Trevor stated.

'Hence the music,' said Edgar. 'You hear it and it's like being born. There's this one song drawn from a Spencer County coal heap ... I want to make something bigger than little rock music medicine bundles for people's living rooms. Gotta do something different. I find a better path in the songs that Dad picks out.'

'Dickie Haughman,' hollered Hector.

'And just listen to the riff,' added Edgar. He paused for a moment to take it in himself. 'But this is my work. And you didn't just come to watch me work.'

Jessamyn did not at all agree with Edgar's assessment of their visit. She realized that she was acting as if this man's house was an art gallery, as if his presence was predicated on displaying the things he had made, or was in the process of making. Really, she was coming to meet a friend of a friend, but she was decidedly more interested in the mythic side of the man. The raw materials of the project fascinated her in a way she hadn't anticipated. She couldn't drag her attention away from them, from the numerous questions they provoked. Edgar had transformed cassette tapes into recognizable forms, but what was this mess of oddities to become? And what about the music, the old man in the chair— was that the glue that held all this together? Zappa's mustache an antenna? But she was there to meet the artist, not consider the things he may or may not birth into the world. She paused, lifted her gaze and let it linger over Edgar's bare, somewhat flabby chest. The paler portions of his skin almost glowed against the warm tones of the kimono. He had incredible, well-nourished and cared-for brown hair that fell atop his shoulders in thick waves. *What sort of man was this Hoosier?*

'I'm interested to see what this all becomes,' she said. 'But you are right. You must get tired of all this art talk.'

'I like her,' Edgar said to Trevor. 'You bring the shisha?'

'Shisha?' asked Jessamyn. 'Like hookah?'

'Yeah,' answered Trevor. 'Grabbed the lychee one from that place up in Broad Ripple.' He retrieved the palm-sized foil package from the depths of his pocket.

'No booze out here,' proclaimed Hector.

'He's right,' added Edgar. 'Old Delaware Peters would have told you that.'

'That shit killed your grandmother,' added Hector. He pulled a long drag from his smoke.

'It really did,' said Edgar. He led them back into the living room. He retrieved a hookah case from beneath the coffee table and set it up while Hector changed records to a K-Tel special edition John Williams vinyl and snuffed out his half-finished smoke.

They settled into their respective chairs while Edgar handed over the hookah, the charcoal and the stoking duties of the entire operation to Trevor. Jessamyn had spent some time in hookah lounges and cafés with her cousins up the freeway from her hometown in and around East Dearborn, Michigan. She had enjoyed those nights spent telling family stories and unbelievable tales. She had preferred those memories and those moments to watching her sorority friends get tanked at Bowling Green's student bars; she was never a drinker of alcohol, even in her years during and after college.

Jessmayn assumed Hector had his cigarettes and would not take part. His lack of movement towards the group seemed to confirm it.

To Edgar and Trevor this hookah was a replaced ceremony, for some part of their collective culture had failed them. Drinking was social ritual in the Midwest, and participation was often central to building bonds between very different people. They carried on as if the shisha, central to all this ritual, their ritual, was a drug of sorts. Jessamyn thought it was a small-town Hoosier way of impressing the new gal with a show of cosmopolitanism. The two men moved through the ritual as naturally as her cousins and brother had. So, to Jessamyn, this was a bit of home, the comfort that she often sought without knowing it. She had missed this, the ritual of setting up the hookah, the conversation that would follow.

'What was it that brought you to Indy?' asked Edgar. He slouched over, crossed his legs and pulled the kimono around the curvature of his belly.

'Lab tech specialist job,' she answered. 'I work over at Lily.'

'That can't be all you do in Indy?' Edgar smiled back at her.

She paused for a moment and tried to think of an interest or hobby that took up her free time, but was disappointed to find there were none. 'That's me,' she said, 'I am my job.'

'Do you like that?' Edgar asked.

'Now that you mention it,' she said, 'it sounds sad.'

'It does make me feel sad,' agreed Edgar. 'But the exceptional thing about time, as I've learned through the way I've spent it, is that we can change what we do with it.'

'Except Hector,' said Trevor. He stoked the coals, replaced the cap.

'Thirty-five years,' Hector added.

Jessamyn glanced back at Hector. She fully expected him to finish that thought. Instead he lit a fresh cigarette and took a deep drag from it. He let some smoke blow out of his nose and said nothing.

'Another habit you are damned fine at,' said Edgar. He leaned forward in anticipation of the hookah wand. Jessamyn waited for one of them to clarify.

Trevor got the hookah rolling and handed the wand to Edgar. He explained that Hector had been heading to the same Fountain Square diner for the last thirty-five years. First after his shift at the now long-shuttered Harvester plant, then after the security job he had at the IPL station near Christian Park. While most of the other guys he worked with hit the bars after their shifts, Hector met Edgar at that neighbourhood diner. There they would play chess, drink bottomless diner coffee and buy whatever dinners they could afford. They played chess as it went best with diner coffee and home-style Indiana pie slices. In those moments playing the game, they felt awash in the intellectual ways that kids who had gone to Butler or U Indy had been fortunate enough to enjoy.

Drinking was not something the Moore boys entertained. It had led their ancestors to bad places, places and happenings they didn't talk about much and that they knew better than to open for examination, lest more trouble slip through. Their great-great-grandfather had guzzled a few too many flagons of applejack before turning traitor at Fallen

Timbers and ending up in the same cold ground as the Shawnee and Delaware at Prophetstown. Nowadays, bars and craft breweries and dance halls were the types of places some working folks made money off other, less intelligent working folks. They were generally smarter than all that, Edgar and Hector were, although, in honesty, money was one thing that neither of them had all that much interest in.

The shisha had been burning a for a solid couple of rounds, and the slight head buzz had kicked in for Jessamyn. It occurred to her just at that moment that she had never seen Trevor drink in all the months she had gotten to know him. In truth, she thought he might have been catering to stereotypes he carried with regard to her culture. It dawned on her now that he likely didn't drink because of his friendship with Edgar. She understood, after spending years in Toledo, how rare it was for white people in the Midwest not to partake in booze.

'You rent this place?' Jessamyn asked.

'You dig it?' replied Edgar. He gave her only two quick beats of the song playing behind him to answer before he continued. 'Because the energy is good. And it's one of those quintessential south-side houses.'

'Reminds folks that half of your people came north from the Commonwealth,' Hector added. He was flipping through some records in a small stack he had pulled off the shelf beside him.

'The McConnells of Covington,' added Edgar. He appeared to trail off into his own mind, searching for memories to bend into words. The room went quiet for an almost unfathomably long time. 'I live at the house that Delaware Peters gave me about ten years back. "Nobody owns a thing," he told me. "Renting is the best we can hope for."'

'Gave?' asked Jessamyn.

'Save an old, lonely Indian,' said Trevor, 'and you'd be surprised at what comes out of it.'

'I suppose I did save him,' replied Edgar. He looked over at Jessamyn, who was visibly perplexed. 'I suppose I should tell you the reason a whole nation down Oklahoma way calls me the Etch A Sketch Shaman. Might even help you to understand what comes next.'

According to Edgar, the day of infamy happened way back when the Pacers were still at Market Square Arena. He had been hustling scalped tickets outside the City-County Building right across Alabama Street from the main parking entrance. As far as he could recall, the game was an important one, probably a playoff game or the like, and he had an easy enough time pushing a pair of mid-level tickets to the game for the price of a few fill-ups for the car, and a decent meal with a couple of veggie sides at the city's fanciest steakhouse. Back then, before making regular cash from his Irvington Flea Market booth, those types of days were full of wonder and splendour.

After divesting himself of his tickets, Edgar found himself at the bar in a real classic Midwestern saloon—one with big, swooping wood flourishes and spotless reflective mirrors behind a neatly ordered wall of liquor bottles. While the shit inside them was poison, it had looked near sacrosanct backlit in front of a well-polished mirror. He insisted that if Jessamyn hadn't seen it, she should make the trip. The shrimp cocktail sauce alone was worth it.

Edgar had sat at the bar with his waist-long hair and unkempt beard, not exactly unlike his contemporary self. Well minus the encroaching grey. (Although Jessamyn wasn't sure that she saw much of any of said grey, she agreed nonetheless, and lingered over the thought of a luxurious shrimp cocktail.) Despite not sporting the standard attire for one of Indy's more refined dining establishments, Edgar struck up a conversation with a man in a full suit and his polo-shirt wearing round-faced friend of generous proportions beside him. They got to talking enough to figure each other out, enough to share some honesty.

As it turned out, the polo-shirt wearing guy introduced himself as Delaware Peters, one of the few people still willing to say they were Indigenous in the state named for Indians. He was a descendant of Selwyn Crowfeather, the last of the Turkey Clan medicine men of the Lenape of Indiana. He was the last because it was Selwyn Crowfeather who had sold the *Walum Olum* to a white guy from Kentucky. The surviving Miami and Shawnee of the area got pissed enough to send him on his way along the great White Path. Through Crowfeather's widow and their children, Delaware Peters had inherited the art of drawing. He had just sold the man with him, a car dealer from Akron, a couple of pieces of his work. They were out celebrating the sale. Edgar admitted that he recognized many similarities between his ticket scalping celebration rituals and their meal and libations.

Delaware had told Edgar then and there that blood heritage was one thing, but the gifts of the Creator were another. While Delaware had inherited the fine gift of drawing that once held all the medicine a nation could hope for, all the history of the ancestors, he had always felt the truly strong medicine of his ancestral heritage had passed him by. Delaware explained that he'd had a vision one particularly hot day at Victory Field, eating a pretzel and cheese dip beside the team teepee, that if he ever found the keeper of that medicine, he would pack up and join his Turkey Clan relations down in Oklahoma. He would do so provided that he knew that the shaman he encountered had the means to heal those most in need. Delaware had explained to Edgar that he would know the right man or woman from an image they made. The keeper of the true medicine would produce said image without any coaxing.

Something in Edgar, perhaps his sinuses, irritated by the explosively spicy cocktail sauce, had proclaimed that they should have a draw-off between himself, the bartender and Delaware's customer friend. All of them agreed with the basic premise, but when the bartender, Larry, a Black Commonwealth guy from the near-westside, returned with three Etch A Sketches, Edgar hesitated. He had not seen one of the red-and-grey magic sand toys since his childhood. He was sure this was some sort of set-up to hustle away from him the thirty dollars he still had from scalping tickets. Delaware had, after all, had that sort of all-American used-car salesman air. But Edgar had agreed to go ahead; something inside told him this day would be prodigious.

Edgar explained that, after a brief circle around the drawing game's knobs, he had fallen into a subconscious rhythm. His eyes and fingers followed the revolutions of the red plastic tablet's knobs, the near invisible needle tip cutting through the metallic sand film inside its clear plastic screen. The basketball game on the TVs above him, the sound around him, the scent of his mostly finished food, all disappeared into the focused micro-movements of the needle. Edgar, Larry and the round-faced guy finished their drawings in about a third of an hour while Delaware took in the last quarter of the Pacer's game on the TV above the bar.

All the men finished their work within the closing minutes of the game and were about to be judged when a decidedly overweight man in a Pacers-themed luchador mask, who had previously been heard shouting the name 'El Pacero' in the background, launched a pint glass and plate of chicken wings into the television above them. The shower of glass and sparks and liquid and food scraps had snapped Edgar back to his senses. El Pacero bolted through the restaurant, out the front door and down Illinois Street, chased by a couple of well-built members of the wait staff. Edgar's attention had returned to Delaware, who had become shockingly pale. He was hunched over, clutching his left arm. Each of the other men recognized the seriousness of the moment: Delaware was having a heart attack.

Larry the bartender had leapt over the bar, lifting Delaware and preparing to start chest compressions. Not fully comprehending the situation, Edgar showed his completed work on the Etch A Sketch to Delaware. The man's rolling eyes caught a glimpse of the image: a turkey chasing a possum down Virginia Avenue. Almost instantaneously, Delaware's face regained a healthy colour. He straight-armed Larry, who was approaching to deliver CPR, and sat bolt upright.

'You cured a dying man with a picture on an Etch A Sketch?' Jessamyn sat with the hookah wand in hand.

'That's the shaman part,' Hector pointed out.

'Does that even make sense?' she demanded.

Edgar laughed. 'There are plenty of things that don't make sense. They just are.'

'How do you know that Delaware was cured?' asked Jessamyn.

'Paramedics,' replied Edgar. 'And his doctor called me a few days after the fact.'

'Dr. Nims,' added Hector.

'One of Beech Grove's finest,' clarified Edgar.

'He did some solid work with your Aunt Jenny's gallbladder,' Hector added.

'It was in the *Indy Star*,' said Trevor. 'Edgar was a real famous guy back in the day. For about a minute. Delaware gave him that nickname in the interview, the Etch A Sketch Shaman.'

'And this house,' said Edgar. He took in a huge haul off the pipe and let loose an equally huge plume of smoke. 'But saving the life of one man is just a starting point. We got a whole city that needs a little medicine and whole lot of healing.'

Orange roofed with dirty, stuccoed walls, Peppy Grill huddled beneath an ancient teal sign that declared HAMBURGERS and 24 HRS to the passing traffic of Virginia Avenue. Jessamyn had received a few texts from Trevor to meet him there after work. It had been a few days since their trip to Edgar's place, but she had found herself considering more and more the modern-day shaman she had met. She wondered if these were the roots of what she might call the evangelical aspects of her aunt's beliefs. Holy men, representations of the divine among the bored working classes, focused her in a way she hadn't expected.

Jessamyn had kept her epiphany mostly to herself, so when Trevor messaged her about getting a late breakfast, she had jumped at the chance. She was certain that no one at work would care about questions of divinity or the actions of a working man's artist-shaman. The majority of her co-workers were, like her, transplants, but unlike her, their interest in putting down roots in Indiana was tepid at best. Indiana as a living, breathing place was centred on notions of divinity that arose from the soil. That was clear from the Bible verses and gospel hymns filling the AM airwaves, acting as fodder for the utopian dreams of storied places like New Harmony and Prophetstown.

Trevor was seated in the green vinyl-and-wood booth closest to the door. He had his back to the plate glass window, and slouched just below the announcement BREAKFAST SERVED ANYTIME. From the age and wear of the interior of this small diner, Jessamyn expected it to smell musty and used, like so many of the greasy spoons back in Toledo. Instead, the air held the smell of unending BUNN coffee atop the sweetness of well-rendered fat and the reassuring undertone of bleach. After exchanging niceties with the old man behind the counter, she sat down across from Trevor. He pulled his attention from the book he was reading and welcomed Jessamyn with an unsteady greeting that let her know he was dwelling on something he would have preferred not to think about.

The two exchanged their pleasantries while the man behind the counter distributed to Jessamyn a laminated, single-page menu printed in a microscopic font. Trevor recommended something fried and with home fries once the cook was out of earshot. He coached against hamburgers, which Jessamyn was wary of from the start. Rosana, her younger sister, had gotten fierce food poisoning from a burger at a very similar diner back in Toledo. The age of the advertisement outside combined with the decided lack of attention to the menu indicated that the hamburger was much more of a metaphor for the diner's nature than it was an actual meal option.

Jessamyn asked Trevor if he had heard anything more about Edgar's grand project. She explained her fascination with the drive of a man-of-the-earth to heal an entire city. She sounded more eager than she wanted to, and she rambled on for a solid few minutes before letting Trevor actually answer.

'I'm worried about Edgar,' he offered just as the cook returned with their food. 'I haven't heard from him since we visited. He gets in these spaces.'

'Spaces?' asked Jessamyn.

'Yeah,' said Trevor. 'A couple months back we—me and a cabinet-maker guy I know from Irvington—found Edgar naked, passed out on his living room floor and high as hell on spray paint fumes.'

'Spray paint?'

'He went through a graffiti phase just before the cassette tape phase,' explained Trevor.

'So, he wasn't just huffing the stuff?' she asked.

'Not totally,' Trevor answered. 'But you can't blame him for getting a little more perspective into his medium. Small room, closed windows kind of perspective. Not quite consciously sought after.'

Jessamyn laughed, partially to relieve the tension building in Trevor's voice, partially from a vision of Edgar's naked self, covered in glitter-heavy paint. 'Those mystics, living by their own rules.'

'Wait,' said Trevor, pausing in a moment of revelation. 'You really bought into this shaman thing, didn't you?'

Jessamyn nodded. 'Well, I mean look at him. He saved a man with an Etch A Sketch.'

'You looked it up in the newspaper archives?' he asked.

'I had a co-worker call the library,' she said. 'It's there.'

Trevor shook his head, took a bite of one of his french fries. 'Edgar is as local as you get. He is a real man-of-the-earth. The way that works around here, the way it works for most of the state to at least the Commonwealth—'

'Commonwealth?' asked Jessamyn. She had been hearing the word often enough and had nodded her way through it often enough, but now she found herself wanting to know as much as possible about the vocabulary Trevor and his friends used.

'Kentucky,' clarified Trevor. 'But guys around here, they don't have money or power or property. This is one of those hard facts about Indiana. There are a lot hard-luck folks here for certain. But they got these stories and myths. I swear the university press down in Bloomington put out some big and important book about it. They are just myths for hard times.'

'And you don't believe in them?' asked Jessamyn. She was markedly disappointed in Trevor's tone about this.

'I wouldn't go that far,' he replied. 'But the best storytellers, the real myth makers, like to exaggerate.'

'I see,' said Jessamyn. She felt a pang of annoyance at Trevor. She had wanted to believe in something profoundly divine and spiritual, to find a particle of the unexplainable in a mechanical world, a glimpse into the magic her family had left behind for their American home. She couldn't help but think she had found that in Edgar, in his striking honesty and his supreme individuality.

'I'm not saying I don't believe,' added Trevor after a long pause. 'I just think you shouldn't be looking for proof of a meaningful way of life in the stories of a ticket scalper and flea market salesman turned artist-shaman.'

Jessamyn nodded in agreement, but in his words she sensed less truth than she did the kind of jealousy that arises between men when women cast their affections counter to pre-laid plans.

Jessamyn was into the third frame of her second game of duckpin bowling when she received a text from Trevor. She was out with a group of her fellow lab rats on a work team chemistry-building social. It had been nearly a week since she and Trevor had met up at Peppy Grill. In all honesty, Trevor was less interesting alone and outside of any connection to Edgar. Jessamyn had been for the most part bored during their only trip to Peppy Grill. The outing had felt like work, and the feeling had caused her to take to the habit of returning his messages only after a considerable delay. She could sense, even in the small number of messages they had exchanged over the course of the week, his disappointment in their interactions.

The duckpin bowling social was her first outing with her co-workers, and it was immensely unfulfilling in terms of meaningful or enjoyable company. After just an hour or so at the atavistic bowling alley at the centre of Fountain Square's main commercial hub, she was considering escape. A belligerent middle-aged senior administrator, Becky from Plainfield, was drunk and had started to discuss her reverence for the beliefs and cultures of Muslim peoples. Becky's niece had been to some country-over-there on a mission with their church and did she ever find the people wonderful. Trevor's text came in after Becky proclaimed her dream of visiting Baghdad.

Trevor: At Peppy patio with Hec

Trevor: Care for a game of chess?

Down street. Be there in 10

Jessamyn explained to Becky and her co-workers that she had to send a couple of emails home, that important things had crept up. Despite the sad grimace on Becky's confused face, Jessamyn bolted out of the third-floor bowling alley after changing shoes and assuring the group she was looking forward to seeing their pleasant faces at work in the morning. By the time she hit street level, the sun had set behind the western bank of houses and storefronts. Virginia Avenue pulled her vision arrow-straight to the nearby high rises of Indianapolis's downtown proper. The avenue itself was a gilded pathway of restricted car lanes, broad bike lanes, and wide sidewalks that culminated in a pinpoint at the base of the distant Chase Tower. The streetlights and backlit signs of the neighbourhood and city around it burned like restless fireflies. A steady stream of early Thursday night car traffic met and flowed around the triangle of an intersection that centred on the ornate fountain that gave the area its name. Jessamyn had thought it odd to name one of the city's more prominent neighbourhoods after such a diminutive piece of public art. Yet, she also found it in keeping with the Hoosier way of celebrating the small, the beautiful, the often overlooked. It was charming.

The brief three-block walk brought her to the weathered wood fence that separated the patio of Peppy Grill from the sidewalk. It was just wide enough at this point for two four-seat tables—the basic Walmart plastic kind—and their chairs. On the far side of the furthest table sat Trevor and Hector. The light from the restaurant sign and a nearby streetlight did a surprisingly fine job illuminating the immediate area around them. Between them was a chessboard, well-used and inexpensive. She could smell Hector's cigarette smoke well before she had realized it was him that was smoking. A half-drunk coffee and mostly eaten sugar pie slice rested next to him.

Jessamyn settled into an empty chair between the two and looked down at the board. They exchanged the quick pleasantries that accompanied expected guests. Hector spoke briefly about the general pleasantness of the evening before turning his full attention back to the chessboard. Jessamyn had no idea who was winning or losing; she rarely came across devout chess players either at home or here in Indy. She imagined the goings-on of the game were similar to a religious ceremony, with each move carefully considered in the manner of older men who passed their nights in cafés and diners.

Trevor remained quiet, focused and serious in a way that Jessamyn had not seen in him before. Perhaps he was winning. Perhaps he was just trying to keep from losing.

'What you doing before this?' asked Hector.

'Duckpin bowling,' she answered.

'You mean duckpin drinking,' Hector said. A crackling laugh emerged from his nearly non-existent belly.

Jessamyn grimaced a smile. She figured Hector's words were like his movements, mainly repeated out of ritual. 'My co-workers were not exactly my cup of tea,' she said.

'Good on you,' he answered. He watched as Trevor used a knight to take out a rook. 'You will live longer, maybe. Maybe have less regrets.' He pulled a long haul off his cigarette, pushed the smoke up to catch the light of the sign above them.

They passed the next hour with the occasional move of a chess piece, arguments over whether Chet Atkins was the best guitarist of his time and discussions about how all the really great country players were born no further north than Brown County, leaving Indy to the mainstream hacks that record labels dumped on witless northerners. Unlike the first time Jessamyn met Hector, he was bright and engaged, like a barred owl at dusk. Freed from his son's record collection, Hector immersed himself in the world and his immediate surroundings with a vigour that Jessamyn had rarely seen in a man his age. Although she did not dare hazard a guess at his actual age, she could tell that there had been a harshness to the years that had deposited this leatherback man before her. Those same hard years no doubt taught him to think deeply over each move in the chess game.

Hector looked over at Jessamyn, eyes burning from behind the tip of his lit cigarette, and took in as much of her as he could before sending his bishop back across the board. He stated that he had known Trevor for years, played him enough times at Peppy that he could dance around him by now. Hector knew Trevor's deal, understood just why he had any care at all for Chet Atkins and chess and his shaman son. Trevor's innate respect for life's gifts had led him here. But Jessamyn was new and strange, and Hector figured that she should enlighten him as to why she would leave a bunch of her peers to come watch two run-of-the-mill Hoosiers plays chess and eat diner food.

Jessamyn stared at the taillights disappearing along the distant end of Virginia Avenue before she replied. The quiet electric hum of the Indiana night, with the leisurely and very occasional passing of cars, had lulled her into an unfamiliar slowness. She had come to accept and field questions of identification on a regular basis, especially since moving to Indiana. This was still post-9/11 America, in the heartland of the country, and her skin tone and looks suggested to many white Americans that, even on the simplest level, she had something to do with the ways their world was changing. On the occasions she was called to explain her background, she was on the one hand completely perturbed, but on the other hand relieved to be given the chance to provide a palatable answer. She even looked and dressed like many of them. She was annoyed that she could so easily sum up all of who she was in some quick, on-demand accounting to a suspicious neighbour or acquaintance. They would allow nothing to be said about her grandparents who had emigrated to Detroit in the 1960s for line work at Chrysler's, nothing about religion and miracles and the politics that had been anything but at the forefront of any part of her life. She would want to explain it all as a way to fit in.

She sensed something in Hector's question that was more sincere than the typical inquisition. It was partially curiosity, but it was also his way of looking to connect with someone who had appeared to be vastly different from himself. It was a shot across the divide. It was the opening that she had sought out countless times before. All of this came together to explain why she found herself watching two Hoosiers moving chess pieces around after dark on the south side of Indianapolis, Indiana. But she also realized that all that backstory didn't matter to Hector. 'Because this place and all of your company makes me feel right,' she said.

The day was heavy and thick with the humidity of the White River flood plain. It clung to the tangle of vines and ditch weeds that sprouted in abundance between the houses on Pleasant Street. It had been nearly a week since Jessamyn, Trevor and Hector had met at Peppy Grill.

Jessamyn had taken a half-day after receiving a message from Trevor that Edgar was unveiling his finished work to his close friends that afternoon. He told her that she had an official invite from Hector, so it must have been important because Hector really only called on family and direct relations.

Her co-workers were a lot less sad at her leaving this time.

Jessamyn crested the stairs, which appeared all the more weathered in broad daylight. She heard the steady strumming of country rock. A note taped to the door invited her to come in and informed her that Rik Smits was in the garage. She recognized the very European name from somewhere around town. In brackets below, the sign instructed her to walk through the kitchen.

Jessamyn entered a house devoid of people. In the corner, the familiar record player was belting out a song about being blue. She called hello a few times and, hearing no response, proceeded into the living room. She looked for motion or any sign of human presence.

From the music playing to the atmosphere inside, the house felt very recently vacated. The album cover was left flat on the chair that had been inhabited by Hector on her previous visit. On it the name Blankenship Brothers hung beneath the black dress pants of five very clean-cut bola-wearing men. The top of the cover declared them the 'Blue Grass and Rockabilly Kings of Indiana'. Jessamyn wouldn't have pictured Hoosier royalty resembling this clear echo of the late 1950s. The essence of things changed rather slowly.

She walked through the cluttered, retro kitchen to a very aptly fading soundtrack. The music ceased behind the closing screen door, and she was left with the boisterous songs of wrens and sparrows and the muffled sounds of men talking in the large garage at the rear of the property.

Inside the two-car garage she found Edgar standing in his familiar kimono beside a very tall upper-middle-aged Scandinavian-looking man, calmly discussing what appeared to be a very serious issue. Hector sat in a lawn chair off to the side, smoking a fresh cigarette and quietly taking in the discussion.

In the middle of the garage sat a classic 1970s AMC Pacer. She had recognized the make and model as one of her uncles had driven a similar car around the streets of Toledo until well into the late 1990s. But this car was covered in the canvas and paints she had seen on the tables inside the house. The skin of the car looked alive. Bald, possum-like in places. Yet there was a reflective glitter to it as if it were the anchor at the end of a rainbow.

Jessamyn had only two words for it: organic and sublime.

'Uh,' she said as both Edgar and the other man turned to face her. 'You left the record on.'

'Blankenship Brothers,' blurted out Hector. 'They recorded over on Spruce.'

'Didn't you date one of their sisters?' asked Edgar.

'I did,' proclaimed Hector with clear pride in his voice. 'Left it on for you,' he told Jessamyn. 'Those some good Fountain Square boys. Better start learning about where you are sinking your roots.'

'Good, I am glad we're not alone to witness this moment,' said the tall fair-haired man.

Edgar briskly introduced the man as Rik, a former basketball pro and an old buddy from Edgar's ticket-scalping days. He was a racing and vintage car aficionado who had donated the car for this project.

'Just what are you going to do in that ...' She trailed off, trying to find a respectful choice of word for the car.

'Possum car,' Rik proudly proclaimed. He had a touch of an accent, but Jessamyn couldn't place its origins. 'The vision came to him in a dream. I think it looks great.'

Jessamyn nodded in agreement. The car did look like some fantastical possum. It was shatteringly lifelike, just as Edgar's take on Zappa's mustache had been. She was duly impressed on one level and nearly horrified on another. 'The possum car is just a part of the whole thing, I gather.'

'You're right,' Edgar began, but he was interrupted by the chime of a cellphone. Hector picked up the phone. He read the message on the screen and hollered that Trevor would be a minute as he was hunting for parking. 'The possum car is the artist part,' continued Edgar.

'So, the other part is the shamanic?' she asked.

'Yes,' said Edgar. 'We have the Etch A Sketch connected to a cellphone in the car.'

'What are you healing, exactly?' asked Jessamyn.

Rik looked at her, perplexed. 'New arrival?' he asked Edgar, who nodded. 'Jeff Foster was like that, too. Always seeing the good.'

'The city is nothing but hard living for a lot of regular folks,' Edgar said. 'Lots of factories and good-paying jobs gone, lots of things we used to make, gone, lots of money we never had, still gone.'

'There are camps of homeless people under the bridges along the White River,' offered Rik.

Jessamyn hadn't been looking for or at the underbelly of her new home. Indiana had seemed very much like the places she had grown up. But for the first time she realized that the world inhabited by Edgar and Hector was decidedly less full of the chattel her degree and her corporate job afforded her. From the possum car to the house Edgar had been gifted to the assortment of records inside, their lives had been stitched together with their own labour and what had been given to them freely. Jessamyn could tell from the whiteness of his smile down to the crispness of his jeans that Rik was as much of a tourist here as she was. He had done well as a professional basketball player, and yet he was here. She found comfort in that.

'Right,' she said, 'I hear you. How you going to do that?'

'We've mapped out the drawing I did to save old Delaware,' said Edgar. 'Following the streets of the city, I'm going to draw that picture on the city itself and on the Etch A Sketch.'

'One of my friends does the computer stuff really good,' said Rik. 'He did a whole cellphone GPS mixer we have connected to the car.'

'Got it mapped out to about an hour to get done,' said Edgar.

The door between the backyard and the garage opened, and Trevor entered. 'Stopped the Blankenship Brothers on my way through the house,' he announced. He and Rik exchanged very familiar and muted greetings. 'Car looks great,' he offered, taking a spot close enough to Jessamyn to afford a more affectionate greeting while maintaining an awkward amount of distance between them.

Edgar took off his kimono, retrieved an old work shirt with the name Pete embroidered across the breast pocket, and pulled it on unceremoniously. He jumped into the car and fired up the ignition with a raspy metallic coo. Rik walked to the back of the garage and opened the ancient double doors to the cracked, weed-infested pavement of the alley. Everyone except for Hector followed the car into the alley.

'Proud of you, son,' Hector hollered from his chair.

'Time to rattle these possum white walls over some brickyard roadways,' offered Edgar through the lowered driver's side window. 'Gotta get this city to a better place.' His voice carried the weight of his will, a will that was untamable, wild at heart, like a tree stand on a vacant lot, full of the feral Indiana that wouldn't die.

Jessamyn knew that Edgar Moore would do exactly what he set out to do. She believed. She stood beside Trevor, close enough to actually smell a hint of sweetness from his deodorant. This was new, and it caught her by surprise. They both watched, with Rik towering behind them, Hector smoking his cigarette in a lawn chair, as Edgar glided the possum car down the alley and coaxed it into a soft right-hand turn onto Spruce Street. It disappeared behind a chain-link fence and then the house at the block's end.

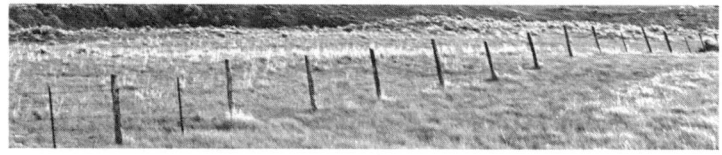

ACKNOWLEDGEMENTS

I would like to thank Don Belton, Tony Ardizzone and Maura Stanton for the years of guidance and mentorship they provided during my time in Indiana. The stories contained in this collection are filled with thankful reflections of the numerous amazing people with whom I forged lifetime friendships during our tenure in the Hoosier state, including Christina Hatton, Chad Thompson, Jonathan Mullens, Mary Beth Mullens, Corina Prather, David Schmid, Elvis Mires, Dave Coonce, Kate Dougherty, Toby Merida and the many others who made our time at the crossroads of America so magical. They are the life-blood that flows through these stories and this book as a whole.

I also wish to thank my fellow writers and workshop survivors who poured over early versions of some of these stories. Catalina Bartlett, Patrick Coleman, Michael Manis, Julianna Crespo, Rachel Lyons, Ashley Ritter and Sana Younis, I thank you for your guidance.

Thanks to my absolutely amazing editor, Stephanie Small, without whom this book would not have been possible.

I would also like to extend my most sincere gratitude to Sharon Berg at *Big Pond Rumours*, who published 'From the Banks of Jeffersonville' in their Summer 2019 issue.

And as always, I would like to thank my wife, Emily, and my daughter, Eleanor. They are the turtle shell upon which my world and this work are built.

ABOUT THE AUTHOR

D. A. Lockhart is the author of eight books, including *Tukhone: Where the River Narrows and the Shores Bend* (Black Moss Press, 2020) and *Devil in the Woods* (Brick Books, 2019). His work has appeared in *Best Canadian Poetry in English 2019*, *TriQuarterly*, *ARC Poetry Magazine*, *Grain*, *Belt* and the *Malahat Review* among many others. He is a Turtle Clan member of Eelünaapéewi Lahkéewiit (Lenape), a registered member of the Moravian of the Thames First Nation and currently resides at the south shore of Waawiiyaatanong (Windsor, ON–Detroit, MI) and Pelee Island. He is the publisher at Urban Farmhouse Press and the poetry editor for the *Windsor Review*.